The Bedford Competition
Anthology 2023

Featuring stories by:

Chris Belson, Joy Clews,
Tony Durrant, Issac Hogarth, David Joseph,
Dell Kaniper, Daniel Key, Sheila Killian,
Felicity Reid, Victoria Stewart, Josie Turner,
James Watson, Lucia Wilde, Gwen Williams

**and
poems by:**

Adam Ali-Hassan, Anne Atkins,
Jeanette Burney, Mark Fiddes, Ben Howard,
Amy Levitin Graver, Lois P Jones,
Stephanie Powell, Gina Shaffer, Kevin Smith,
Ben Verinder, Louise Walker, Donald Wildman

Published in paperback by
The Bedford Competition Ltd

First published in Great Britain 2024

Copyright ©

Adam Ali-Hassan, Anne Atkins, Chris Belsen, Jeanette Burney, Joy Clews, Tony Durrant, Mark Fiddes, Amy Levitin Graver, Isaac Hogarth, Ben Howard, Lois P Jones, David Joseph, Dell Kaniper, Daniel Key, Sheila Killian, Stephanie Powell, Felicity Reid, Gina Shaffer, Kevin Smith, Victoria Stewart, Josie Turner, Ben Verinder, Louise Walker, James Watson, Lucia Wilde Donald Wildman, Gwen Williams assert the moral right to be identified as the authors of this work.

This anthology is entirely a work of fiction. The names, characters and incidents portrayed in it are the work of the authors' imaginations. Any resemblance to actual persons, living or dead, events or localities is entirely coincidental.

All rights reserved. No part of this publication may be reproduced, stored in, or introduced into a retrieval system, or transmitted, in any form, or by any means (electronic, mechanical, copying, record or otherwise) without the prior permission of the author or authors. Any person who does any unauthorized act in relation to this publication may be liable for criminal prosecution and civil claims for damages.

This book is sold subject to the condition that it will not, by way of trade or otherwise, be lent, resold, hired out or otherwise resold without the authors' prior consent in any form other than that in which it is published and without a similar condition, including this condition, being imposed on the subsequent purchaser.

ISBN: 979-8-3214004-7-0

Typesetting by Elaine Sharples

Cover design by Roberto Andrade of
Box Monster Promotions

Foreword by the Chair of The Bedford Competition
Frank McMahon

My sincere thanks go to all who made this year's competition a resounding success. With the standard of entries higher than ever, our judges rose to the challenge of selecting outstanding stories and poems from over 2000 submissions. Their skill is much admired and appreciated. A special thank you must go to all our readers for their time and effort in helping in the initial stages of judging. Their support over the years has unquestionably enabled the competition to go from strength to strength.

With entries from over thirty countries, exceeding expectations, we have been able to make significant donations to our chosen charities for this year: Bedford and District Palsy Society; International Refugee Trust; Ridgeway School.

It has been a great privilege to read this year's entries which give insight into the wealth of talent and ability from around the world. The many poems and stories in this anthology reflect the ingenuity and imagination of so many writers. I hope that you too will appreciate and enjoy this year's offerings.

Finally, particular thanks to my colleagues Philip Carey, Marie Coles, Nicola Darwood, Sarah Davies, Marjorie Fitt, Maureen Hanrahan, Rosalina Lionetti, Paul Moss and Veronica Sims for all their hard work and dedication. Thanks also to the many local groups and individuals for their continuing help and support.

Contents

Foreword by the Chair of The Bedford Competition
Frank McMahon iii

2023 SHORT STORY COMPETITION 1
Short Story Competition Judge's Report Tim Jarvis 3
Joey Isaac Hogarth FIRST PRIZE 5
Church Going Victoria Stewart SECOND PRIZE 17
Inner Loop Josie Turner THIRD PRIZE 25
All Business James Watson 33
A dying breed Tony Durrant 41
Hide Chris Belson 49
Home Turf Joy Clews 55
I Wanted to be a Bluesman David Joseph 61
A Song from a Different Room Gwen Williams 69
Starfish Sheila Killian 77
Sunday Morning Dell Keniper 85
Thomas and Will Felicity Reid 93

2023 CYGNATURE SHORT STORY PRIZEWINNER 103
Cygnature Short Story Prize Judge J S Watts 105
One Last Dream Daniel Key 109

2023 BEDFORD SHORT STORY PRIZE WINNER 117
Bedford Short Story Prize Judge's Report Paul Barnes 119
The Truffle Hunters Lucia Wilde 121

2023 POETRY COMPETITION 129
Poetry Competition Judge's Report Kirsten Norrie 131
PANTOUM (after Béla Tarr) Ben Howard FIRST PRIZE 135
Counter Meals Stephanie Powell SECOND PRIZE 137

Ode to a Chimú Pot Mark Fiddes THIRD PRIZE	139
Ars Poetica: 6pm Louise Walker	140
Autumn Wind Jeanette Burney	142
COLOR BLIND Gina Shaffer	143
End of an Afternoon Donald Wildman	144
Homecoming Amy Levitin Graver	145
Otsuchi Ben Verinder	146
Life in a Hammershøi Painting:A study of parts Lois P Jones	147
Mythology Ben Verinder	149
A RIVER RUNNING SHALLOW Kevin Smith	151
2023 CYGNATURE POETRY PRIZEWINNER	153
Cygnature Poetry Prize Judge's Report Sarah Davies	155
Ashur Acha Iddina Adam Ali-Hassan	159
2023 BEDFORD POETRY PRIZE WINNER	161
Bedford Poetry Prize Judge's Report Liam Coles	163
Mothering Sunday: At the "Garden of Rest" Anne Atkins	165
Biographies	167
The Bedford Competition 2024	178

2023 SHORT STORY COMPETITION

Short Story Competition Judge's Report
Tim Jarvis

The short story is a compelling, unique form, and quite distinct from longer prose fiction. One of the main things I was looking for when reading competition entries was a sense of that difference, an understanding of the particular features that make a tale work. As Joyce Carol Oates puts it, short stories require 'a concentration of imagination, and not an expansion'. While novels might deal primarily in character and narrative, the most important elements of a story are a compelling architecture, an immersive atmosphere, and taut prose.

The most obvious shape for narrative is an arc or wave moving from equilibrium to disequilibrium and back to equilibrium again. This can be powerful in longer stories but doesn't tend to work as well in a tale. A common form, with a similar structure, which does work well in shorter pieces, is the transformation of a character's attitude or way of thinking following an epiphany or revelation of some kind, but this can feel a little tired, unless revived in some way. Story structures need a quirk of some kind. As Ra Page describes it: 'All short stories have a flaw. Deep in their programming, coiled in their moment of conception, there's a glitch. A bad command-string. A contradiction.'

And I was on the lookout, when reading through, for entries that did inventive and original things with structure, that sought out unusual or different shapes—for those flaws, those glitches.

Atmosphere, or what Edgar Allan Poe called 'unity of effect', is also crucial, so I was also reading aware to the kinds of moods the tales conjured, looking for subtlety and expressiveness of tonal palette.

And language really is at the fore of the art of the short story, what Malcolm Bradbury called 'its linguistic and stylistic concentration, its imagistic methods, its symbolic potential.' So those stories that stood out to me were those where the prose was focussed on the creation of powerful poetic effects, which took risks with word choice and syntax, that were scaffolded with rich symbolism.

So I had a keen eye for these three aspects as I read through the stories and whittled them down to a short list. Which was by no means an easy feat—the overall quality of the submissions I read was really high, and they were all inventive—there was very little reliance on stock tropes and situations. It was also amazing to see such a diversity of approach and cultural context—which kept the reading fresh and engaging.

But the stories on the short list all have something special about them, are all structurally and linguistically playful and inventive, and give us a glimpse into another world. There are stories that inhabit the minds of characters with a unique perspective, and stories which give us cruelty and also hope. There are stories that weave the historical and the fictional with a light touch and offer alternative versions of well-known events. There are also stories of small-town bleakness, and redemption found in art.

So, it says something that the top three stories stood out from even this excellent set. In third place is *Inner Loop* by Josie Turner. This story has a powerful structural conceit, a narrator trapped by guilt over a blind eye maybe turned to an act of violence in a psychological inner loop that mirrors the outer inner loop seen from her hotel room. It has nuance, a rich and convincing voice, and an ending that gives the reader a shudder.

In second place is *Church Going* by Victoria Stewart. This vicious Gothic tale simmers with violence, betrayal and vengeance, but it's a nastiness buried beneath an elegant and subtle surface. Another tale with a clever structural conceit, moving inexorably towards a revelation that forces you to reconsider the narrator and everything you've read, a brutal ending that takes your breath.

And in first place is Isaac Hogarth's story, *Joey*. The poignancy of this tale of a young girl's loss and grief is remarkably untouched by mawkishness or sentiment—when the narrator climbs into the makeshift kangaroo pouch she has sewn from her mother's things, it is genuinely heartrending. This story does all the things I was looking for in my judging—it is structurally inventive, fully immersive, and the writing is lyrical, experimental, and rich in poetry.

SHORT STORY FIRST PRIZE

Joey
Isaac Hogarth

Dad long dead now too, but I remember sitting in his lap out on the wraparound porch and shining a flashlight out into the dark of the paddock. Dozens of kangaroos stood taxidermy-still in the beam, stuffed with cotton and their insides somewhere long gone or ground into dog food. Behind them, the glowing ovum of the moon breaching the tall grass and spinning disc-like in the fluid gloom. Dad ruffling my hair in his fingers. The joeys wriggling lumpish in their mumma's pouches.

it must be so comfy in there

                                      maybe i'll trade you
                             i bet a joey's got less attitude

what's an attitude

                                          it's what you've got

no i don't

                                            see, right there

Then it was usually dinner, and it was usually in front of the TV. We watched free-to-air and ate chicken and green beans. From outside we could hear the demon song of the mating possums, the shrieking and the hissing. The cricket's crying metronome. There was a dog snoring at my feet. He was a mutt but must've been mostly cattle dog on account of the blueish coat and the big sad head. He was skinny for an old boy and covered in warts. He was called Skink, cuz he was always eating little lizards he found. I remember pushing my toes through his fur, poking them into his soft warm belly.

When dinner was done, I liked to go right back to the porch. Over the years it had started to slump over so anything you dropped would roll away from you. I gripped the flashlight tight. Dad came and ruffled my hair. He let me sip his beer, but I didn't like it.

yuck

                                      beer's like back pain
                           you'll only get it when you're older

I stared out into the field, holding my eyes open with my fingers, trying to resist closing them. The flashlight balanced in my lap. I was looking at a roo. It was looking back at me.

                                      why aren't you blinking

it's a staring contest

                                  you're gonna lose that game
                                                roos don't blink

My eyes dried out in the summer night heat. I had to blink. Then everything was blurry and wet. Smudged stars floating in black water. The cardiac moon pulsing and the glow-like blood flowing in the pale veins of the Milky Way and dripping down into the world and pooling silver in the eyes of the kangaroos. But they kept staring. They never blinked.

In the morning, we drove into town with Skink in the backseat. I hung my head out the passenger window. Beside the tarmac there was always kangaroo roadkill in various states of decomposition. Some just looking like they were sleeping funny. Some with their stomachs eaten away and their jagged ribs clawing upward. Once, I saw a roo splayed out Christlike and its guts hanging limp out its opened belly. Blood hissed and congealed on the boiled blacktop. Other roos stood around with their heads down like some strange roadside funeral.

do animals get sad when
somebody dies

                                                          of course

is that why Skink

is so sad

                                              how do you mean

cause he misses Mum

                              Skink's always been a sook

*

I remember one night better than some others. For dinner Dad roasted potatoes and carrots and a big hunk of beef. By the time Dad finished his food, I had barely touched mine.

                                                        eat up

i'm not hungry

                                    you're always hungry

why don't kangaroos blink

                                      i'm not sure of
                              the science of it exactly

is it cuz they don't wanna miss anything

                                                  go on
                                               eat up

When the dishes were done, I went right back out to the porch and flicked on the flashlight. But there was nothing out there. Dad came and ruffled my hair.

is the flashlight broken

                                                                no

then where did all the roos go

                                    i dunno sweetheart
                             probably got sick of you
                      shining that thing in their eyes

I moved the flashlight's beam slowly across the paddock. Nothing out there, nothing at all. Then Dad grabbed my hand and held it still. It took a moment, but I saw it. There was a roo laying on its side, facing away from us. Dad sighed and kissed me on the forehead.

its sleeping

                                                                                                    no

                                                                   roos are nocturnal baby

what does that mean

                                                    they only sleep in the daytime

like you sometimes

                                                                                         sure

can we go look at it

                                                                    it's dead baby

can we go look at it

                                                                                         sure

    Skink came with us. The dead roo in the flashlight's blinding halo, getting closer and closer. Its fur was matted and wet and wine stained. Skink sniffed the corpse then prostrated beside it in mourning. Dad kept his hand on my head. The flashlight making the blood sparkle like the deep red starry sky of another world. Dad took me around to the front side of the roo, where it lay facing toward the moon. Its eyes were wide open and empty. Bulging belly slick with black blood and something else; the sticky sheen of saliva. There was a strange growth on the lower stomach, just below the pouch. This pale pink lump, the size of a little toe. But the lump was moving. I knelt down to get a closer look. The lump shivered and crawled toward the pouch. In the flashlight's beam it became transparent. Golden veins woven throughout its blank body. A shrunken heart thumping darkly like a shivering pebble. It had no eyes, no ears, nothing at all but new flesh and the beginnings of bones thinner than hairs.

                                                                     poor thing

what is it

                                                                       newborn

what's it doing

                                                    trying to get to the pouch

don't move

                                                 where are you running to

I ran back to the house and grabbed one of my t-shirts. When I returned, I reached down to where the newborn clung to its mother. It resisted with the little strength it had, but it was no use; I pried it away like peeling a scab.

>baby
>don't do that

I laid the newborn down inside the shirt and then bundled it up, doing my best to create a pouch. The creature was shuddering. I hurried back inside and sat by the radiator with the pouch in my lap, trying to keep the newborn warm. Dad was shaking his head, ruffling my hair.

>it's not gonna work like that, sweetie
>it's too young
>it needs a mother

no it doesn't

>let's take it to the vet
>if you really want to give it a go

i can do it
i'm gonna call it Bunny
cuz kangaroos look like
big rabbits

>darling
>don't do that

go away

>sweetheart

leave me alone

Dad sighed and watched me for a minute. Then he went to his room. I sat there by the radiator with the pouch in my lap. Now and then I peeked inside, just to check that the newborn was still wriggling around. Skink was curled up beside me and snoring or whining. I knew he was dreaming about her. I knew cuz of the way his eyelids moved.

I tried to stay awake, tried to fight off the dreams, but they got me in the end. I dozed off with the shirt in my lap, the newborn shivering within. I dreamt that I was deforming. My hair uprooting and drifting away like the florets of a dandelion. My skin peeling back, revealing a pure, clammy substance beneath. Eyelids closing slow, then becoming sealed shut. Ears like spools of flesh furling inward until they had degenerated entirely, until they were just two holes either side of my featureless head. I was a newborn roo. Eyeless and glossy pink. Blue heart the size of a baby tooth. Warm and safe in my mother's pouch. Asleep, deep asleep.

*

When I woke up, I rubbed my eyes till they started to hurt, to make sure they were still there. Then I peeked into the pouch. The newborn had stopped shivering. It had turned white. I don't know when it died, could've been anytime during the night. Only seeing it perfectly still did I realise how much it had been quaking and contorting when it was alive; now it was limp and shapeless, like a substance that a cat might vomit up. I shone the flashlight on it. Glowing veins spiderwebbing through its pale body, leading mazelike to the tiny blue heart now unbeating. I sat there staring at that stagnated heart for I dunno how long.

Eventually, Dad woke up and he kissed me on the forehead and took the pouch from my arms. He disappeared outside for some time. Then he came back and sat with me. Kissed me on the top of the head and whispered into my hair.

it's okay baby

I was crying. I looked into the pouch, where it hung half-open in his grip. It was empty.

*

I got Dad to teach me how to use the sewing machine. He took great care with it, cuz he was afraid I would stitch my fingers together on accident or something.

i know someone

> who got her hair stuck
> in a sewing machine
> can you guess who

I spent my days stitching together blankets with red flanelettes from the kitchen and Dad's T-shirts and Mum's old dresses. Dad asked me what I was doing. I never answered him. I started not talking much at all.

> sweetheart
> this isn't like you
> please tell me what's going on

When I wasn't at the sewing machine I was sitting with Skink amongst the kangaroos, all of us lazing about in the sun. I looked closely at the joey's poking their heads out their mum's pouches. Some were hairless with fresh eyes only just opened, red-irised with shiny oil slick pupils and a cloudy blueish film. Some without eyes at all, only dark spheres developing under a thick, half-transparent pinkish membrane. I cried watching them and I didn't know why.

*

One morning, Dad drove us into town to visit Mum. I sat with my head out the window. The sky above was blue forever, like how it must've looked before clouds ever first gathered. The farmland was all wrong, though. Everything deeply tanned, burnt, waiting to burn. This motherless expanse of brown or yellow grass, sheep standing in ritual formation trying to summon just a drop of rain, black horses hooded with fly masks and the midges swarming locust-like.

The roadside was littered with kangaroo corpses festering in the jaundiced sunlight. Too many to count. And the living gathered around and leaning back on their tails with their ears down and their arms hanging forward with hands almost folded together. The dead with concaving flesh and their bones crushed. I wondered if there were joeys in their bleeding pouches. Dad was talking.

> need to take Skink to the vet
> cuz he's got a lump
> and it feels funny

We left flowers on her grave and stood a while staring into the ground. On a hill overlooking the cemetery a mob of kangaroos were grazing. Butcherbirds were perched upon headstones like small spirits in monochrome. Sunshine came down as a fall of bright white rain and gathered blindingly in reflective surfaces, car mirrors going by in flashes of light and street signs flickering candlelike. I felt Dad squeeze the back of my neck gently. He knelt down and turned me to look at him. There were tears painting dark trails down his face.

> it's just you and me
> we won't make it
> if you don't talk to me

But I didn't know what to say. I didn't have the words for it yet. On the drive home Dad wouldn't let me turn on the radio.

> if you're not gonna say anything
> then you'll have to deal with the silence

The world out the car window was bright and sickly. The harsh sunlight seemed to make it featureless, flat and blank. The trees and the hills shrouded in glare. The blacktop twinkling and bubbling, slick with bone dry glow. Dad's face painted by the sun pouring through the windshield, his nose and eyes and mouth vanishing in a tide of blinding light. I longed for somewhere dark, far away from the sun, somewhere small and comfortable where the light can't get in. I closed my eyes and imagined I was there.

*

Dawn came just as I finished up at the sewing machine. I'd used up two blankets, four flanelettes, three of dad's shirts, six of mum's dresses, three pairs of my socks, and the insoles from a pair of Mum's gumboots. They were stitched together haphazardly in a shape like a big sleeping bag; a rounded space that I could crawl into. I dragged it outside to the porch. It had a strange weight to it, despite being made up of things which were soft and thin. Skink came with me. Dad wasn't awake yet. There was a mob of roos in the field. I went toward them.

A joey was hopping circles around its mother. It was still hairless but had eyes and ears and everything else. When it saw me coming over, it climbed into its mother's pouch. She stood, watching me with these big black eyes like spheres of harvested night. The joey poking its tiny head out and squinting. I laid it on the ground. This hollow I had sewn together from so many gentle things. I crawled inside. Skink came in too.

Pitch black and swimming with a kind of organic heat. This membrane I had built for myself. I knew the kangaroos were gathered around, but I couldn't feel their staring. I was in my own edgeless reality, far away from them. Skink liked it. He could smell Mum in her clothes. I could as well if I focused. But I didn't know what the smell was called. I just called it Mum.

Felt a hand pressing through the fabric of the pouch and caressing me. I wriggled around, trying to shake off reality, but the hand found me no matter where I moved within the darkness. It stroked my hair through the coarse material of a tea-towel.

                                                      baby
                                  what're you doing

i'm a joey

I heard a rumble, a sound like the sky cracking open, the omen of lightning. In the world beyond the pouch there was a storm brewing, the first there'd been for a long time.

                                is Skink in there with you

i can't hear you

                                             yes you can

i don't have ears or eyes yet

                                             yes you do

Then the rain came, the wet stampede. Dad sighed. The green smell of damp soil found its way into the pouch. I blocked my nose to it.

can i come in
i'm getting soaked out here

I didn't say anything. Dad sighed again and lifted the pouch open. Grey light spilled inside and gathered palely. Dad's silhouetted portraited in a circular dark. Beyond him were dusk clouds bubbling like raw petroleum, the black rain coming down tarry and heavy. Some found its way into the pouch.

Dad crawled in. Once the opening fell shut behind him, the warm darkness obscured everything once more. I felt him wriggling around, trying to get between me and Skink. He wrapped me in his arms and scratched my head.

don't touch my hair
i don't have hair

you do have hair
you have beautiful hair

no i don't
i'm a joey
in my mummy's pouch
i don't have eyes
i don't have hair
i barely have a heart
of my own

oh darling
i miss her too

We didn't talk for a while. Just the sound of the rain, the many strange whines of Skink's sleep, the thunder here and there. The fabric of the pouch had soaked through. It stuck against me, seemed to fuse coldly with my face. As if it was sewing itself to my skin.

why don't we get out of this thing

it's getting stuffy in here

i'm not ready
i'm still sad

oh sweetheart
it'll always make you sad
but you'll be alright

Skink was the first to leave the pouch. Then I let Dad carry me out. The rain was coming down hard. There were kangaroos stood like statues all around. They had merged with the night, lightless against the burgeoning moonglow besides the soft shimmer of their eyes and the wet sparkle of their dripping fur. Slippery eyes like dark mirrors. They didn't blink. But it was alright.

The pouch was weighed down by the rain it had absorbed. Dad helped me drag it through the field. The kangaroos sinking away into the gloom. Too dark even to see their eyes. Too dark even to see the rain which was falling now with such weight and frequency that it seemed the entire black sky was melting and dripping its cold renderings. We threw the waterlogged pouch over the hills-hoist. Then we went inside.

*

The rain stopped in the middle of the night and by late morning the pouch was already dry. Dad pulled it down from the clothesline. Together we took apart my shoddy work, separated the blankets from the shirts and the dresses and the tea-towels. We put Mum's clothes back in the cupboard. Some of them were torn up but Dad said it was okay.

I sat on his lap out on the porch, the flashlight sun over the world and all of us hypnotised in its beam and dreaming of this strange world where mothers die and roos never blink. There was a mob of them out in the field, lying down or grazing lazily. Skink doddered over and laid down with them. Dad kissed me on the head.

when Skink dies
we should feed him to the kangaroos
he would like that

                                          kangaroos are herbivores baby
what's that mean

                                                          vegetarian
oh

                                                        and anyway
                                                    when Skink dies
                                      we'll dress him in human clothes
                                           and bury him next to Mummy

SHORT STORY SECOND PRIZE

Church Going
Victoria Stewart

It was the third church of the day.

As he pulled up on the verge at the bottom of the path, Jamie said, 'We can have a day off churches tomorrow, promise.'

I laughed, as though to imply that I was more than happy to continue going round churches all week if that was the plan. In fact, I'd indeed had enough. At each one, Jamie did his best to communicate enthusiasm for the unique features, the stone font, the original pulpit, the pre-Reformation stained-glass, but I remained untouched. None of those things impressed me as either feats of engineering or works of art, and I didn't feel anything spiritually either. At church number two, that morning, there'd been some frescoes that were more than five hundred years old, but all you could make out were indistinct shapes that reminded me of nothing so much as the stains that'd been left on the kitchen ceiling after the boiler leaked that time.

But we couldn't not have a look at this one. Apparently, it was the only surviving example of Saxon something or other in the county. Or was it the country? Jamie had told us when we were on the way, but I'd tuned out.

As he strode off, Helen linked my arm and said, 'You will say, won't you? You know what he's like, he'd happily spend the whole week going round churches.'

'It's fine,' I said. 'Really. It's just nice to…you know…'

She nodded slowly, as if she did know, and then said, lightly, 'I'm determined to get him to stop at that interiors shop next time we go past.'

The interiors shop didn't really interest me either, but I smiled, and we followed Jamie through the low gate in the hedge. Jamie wasn't religious, but he was an architect and, although as far as I knew he specialised in designing charmless public facilities with slices of bright coloured plastic stuck on the front and asymmetrical windows, he enjoyed looking round old buildings, admired the craftsmanship. Helen liked the social history side of it and spent a lot of time reading the inscriptions on monuments and wondering how someone with a surname like that had ended up here, and saying wasn't it sad that all those children had died so young. I tended to get distracted by things like the single glove left on the back of a pew for the owner to retrieve, the incongruous technicolour posters for Water Aid projects and charity goats, the pathetic, Sunday school pictures blu-tacked up in the darkest corner, Jesus recognisable by the brown crayon lines of his beard, or the comments in the visitors' book, veering between praise for the wonderful atmosphere and complaint about the lack of toilets. All the stuff that just served to pile on the melancholy, that was what I noticed.

But even I could see this one was unusual. The stone arch over the single wooden door was carved in angular patterns, zigzags that had a 1970s look about them. Jamie was saying something about how it was a style that was common in North Africa and how there'd been debate about how it might have happened that workmen in Worcestershire had imitated it. Maybe a North African had found his way here and shown the locals how? I could see what Jamie meant: a memory came to mind of when Sean and I went to Morocco. The tiling in the medieval baths we'd visited had had a design like this.

Jamie said we should have a look at the windows before we went inside, and as I hesitated, about to go to the right, he smiled and said, 'Not widdershins', and set off to the left. I remembered this from another trip we'd had. Apparently, it's bad luck to go round a church anti-clockwise, though I felt like saying to him, it didn't work, did it, following that rule, it didn't save me from bad luck, didn't stop probably the worst thing that could happen from happening. But I remained silent and complied. We edged our way round through the long grass, still wet from the morning's rain. The sun was trying its best in the thin, not-yet-up-to-full-power way of April.

'Each of the windows, they've got the signs of the zodiac carved above them, see?' Jamie said.

Helen was interested by this, asked Jamie if it was surprising that they should appear so early, and in such recognisable form. They walked ahead of me, trying to figure out which was the Archer, which the Water Carrier. The windows were high and the carvings even higher, and I soon got tired of craning to see and wandered off in among the gravestones, very old ones on this side, mossy and illegible, but round the corner there were a few that were much more recent, shiny and black with gold lettering, one with fresh flowers in an urn, the storybook version of a churchyard butting up against the reality of loss.

Or so Helen perhaps thought, because when she saw me looking at those red roses, she came and put her hand on my arm and said, 'Shall we go inside now?'

She said it in the voice that she used, I believed, to indicate to me that she was there if I wanted to talk about how I was feeling. I gave her the weak smile that was intended to communicate that I appreciated the sentiment, and followed her meekly, wondering how she'd react if I did tell her how I was feeling, if I broke our unspoken, unspeakable pact.

Sean wouldn't have liked it, but I gave in to his mother's wish for him to have a grave like those ones, with a black headstone and gold letters. He would have said it was naff, but I decided it was the least I could do for the poor woman, and in any case, didn't have the energy to argue. She seemed to welcome being tasked with organising the funeral; it kept her busy. All I had to do was choose what to wear, get myself there, play the part. The municipal cemetery was a ten-minute drive from her house, and she kept telling me this, that she liked the idea of Sean being close by so that she could go and visit him. Thinking about where he would be laid to rest seemed to distract her from the questions of where he'd been going when he'd crashed and how he'd come to take that stuff that probably made him too drowsy to keep his eyes open. She seemed utterly incurious about that.

With its orderly rows stretching into the distance as far as the eye could see, that cemetery had made me think of a supermarket car park, packed full on a Saturday afternoon.

Helen and I went in. At first, the interior seemed very similar to others we'd seen, not just that day but on other trips like this one: two very short rows of wooden Victorian pews and, at the back, a carved wooden screen, also, I knew even without having been consciously paying attention to Jamie, a Victorian addition. There was no sign that it was in regular use, no hymn books or embroidered kneelers. It was probably the sort of place that only got opened up when someone local decided it'd look good in their wedding photos.

Jamie had walked the three or four paces up the aisle and was looking up at the ceiling. Helen and I looked up as well. Earlier in the day, at church number one, we'd seen an angel roof, the beams carved with wings and faces, impressive for its ingenuity if nothing else, I had to admit, but the vaulting here was stone, and there was none of the fancy carving we'd seen around the doorway or the windows.

It was cold, a damper, more penetrating cold than you'd expect given how relatively mild the day had been.

Jamie was up on the altar now. There was what looked like a plain wooden table in the middle of it, but he seemed to be examining it quite intently, and then he looked up at the ceiling again.

'Come and see this,' he said.

Helen had drifted off towards a memorial tucked away in the corner opposite the door. I walked across the uneven herringboned brick floor and up the steps to see what had caught his eye this time.

There was a large mirror fixed onto the table. The church with the angel roof had had mirrors in a rack by the door, and you could use them to see what was up there without getting a crick in your neck. It was a neat idea, had provided me with two minutes of amusement, not least because those mirrors had reminded me of the ones the hairdresser uses to show you what the back looks like.

This one had a wooden frame and was bolted down at the corners, and at first glance I felt slightly vertiginous, because although the rest of the building was whitewashed and rather bare, the ceiling over the altar was painted in a design that echoed the zigzags around the door, and the colours that had been used, bright red and mustard yellow, seemed unfaded and fresh, so that when I looked into the mirror, for a moment it was as if I was looking down a kaleidoscope. I had to resist the urge to take hold of the edge of the table. The mirror appeared to magnify the image of what was above, and I felt a strong desire to look away.

'What's that all about?' I said. 'Bit brash, isn't it?'

'Like being in a tent, you know, a circus tent, or something,' Jamie said.

I looked up, then looked down again.

'If you stand here,' he said, moving round to where the priest might stand during a service, 'there's…come and see,'

I went and stood next to him.

'See,' he said.

I couldn't see what he meant. The pattern looked the same. He tried pointing and then laughed because of course the reflection of his hand and arm blocked what he wanted to show me.

'Here,' he said, and he moved so that I could stand in the place where he'd been standing, and then the pattern reflected in the mirror suddenly resolved itself into a face, a face with a yellow tongue and eyes, flames licking around it, a huge, disembodied, devilish head.

'Bloody hell,' I said, and he said, 'Well, yeah,' and we both laughed.

'What is it?' said Helen, coming up onto the altar.

I stepped back and let her take my place at the table. She looked, took a moment, as I had, to see what it was, then was as surprised as I'd been.

I was prompted to some mischief.

'You know, Sean, he could never see stuff like that, you know, optical illusions, the duck that's a rabbit, or those magic eye pictures, that's what that reminds me of a bit, he could just never get them to look like anything. But he had astigmatism, I wonder if that was why?'

They fell silent, and then, almost immediately, Helen said, 'Yeah, I remember him saying his contact lenses cost a fortune.'

This was the way of dealing with the situation that we'd evolved now, eighteen months on. We'd reached the stage where it was permissible to mention Sean and for it not to derail the whole conversation. They'd taken the lead from me, of course; of course they had, it was worst for me, and it was only right that I should be the one to set the tone, set the pace, as we advanced through the seven stages of grief. Or was it thirteen? It depended on who you read.

You could argue that it was worse for Helen, if you were in full possession of the facts, as I was. I certainly did my best to make it worse for her, in subtle ways, like making odd comments such as that one about Sean's eyesight, and not so subtle ways, like accepting their invitation to come away on holiday with them, because we could still have fun, couldn't we, even though it was no longer the four of us, just we three?

Jamie had stepped away from the altar table and I saw him looking at the little carved door that led into the pulpit, but he didn't go up there. Perhaps he was remembering that thing that Sean did once or twice when we were in empty churches like this one. He'd go into the pulpit and deliver a hellfire and brimstone sermon, leaning energetically over the lectern, gesticulating and rolling his eyes at an imaginary congregation, inveighing against fornication and scarlet women. Once he adopted a broad Yorkshire accent to do this, another time, an Ian Paisley twang. Sean had been raised Catholic and though he'd given it up when he was a teenager, he found churches of other denominations very stark and plain, no pictures to look at when you got bored, he used to say, and those tatty old military standards, what were they all about, and a church wasn't really a church unless it smelt of incense. In Spain, once, he made obscene suggestions to me in a confessional, him on one side of the grille and me on the other. It was like some low rent porn film but that was the point, it was funny, it was fun. Despite everything, we had a lot of fun, me and Sean.

I couldn't imagine Jamie and Helen making obscene suggestions to each other, whether in a confessional or not. Jamie had always struck me as somewhat sexless; it wasn't just that he did nothing for me in that department, I couldn't grasp what anyone else might see in him either. He was slight, fair, looked like he never needed to shave. Helen, I could see why she might seem appealing, unselfconscious about her height, never flaunting her hourglass figure, but managing to communicate to you that it was there, underneath the hand-knitted-looking jumpers and sensible waterproof coats and straight-legged cords from Marks & Spencer.

Yes, you could see what the deal was with Helen. Sean, he'd evidently seen what the deal was.

I asked him straight out once, not long after he'd introduced me to them, his oldest friends, asked him if he fancied her, if there'd ever been anything between them, and he'd said, God, no, of course not, Helen and Jamie had already been together when he'd first got to know them, they were that mythic couple who met in the queue to register on the first day at university, stayed together and got married a month after graduation.

I didn't press him, but even at the time, it struck me that saying they were already together when he met them didn't quite answer my question.

Helen had led Jamie away from the altar and they were walking down the aisle. She was pointing towards the memorial she'd been looking at earlier. Jamie was on her right. If they'd just got married, he would have been on her left. Was that bad luck, walking down the aisle the wrong way round, like going widdershins?

I drifted back to the altar table. As I approached, the mirror seemed grey and empty. I tipped my head back and looked up at the ceiling, felt that vertiginous rush again, not unpleasant this time. I stepped closer, and the reflection filled the mirror again. Now I was reminded, not that I needed reminding, of the mirror that hung on one of the staircases at that place we'd stayed in Shropshire. That was an old rectory as well, like the place where we were staying. It had a flight of stairs at each side of the sitting room, and we joked that we had a wing each, Helen and Jamie on one side, Sean and me on the other. Except for when I glimpsed Helen, her image in that mirror echoed shadowly in the glass panel of a door down below, and when I crept closer, I caught sight of the reflection of something I wasn't supposed to have seen. There she was on the wrong staircase, the wrong side of the house. There they were.

Bring hellfire raining down on the whore of Babylon, that was the type of thing Sean would say when he was pretending to be a preacher.

I stood on the spot that made the shapes up above resolve themselves into a face. I wondered at the pointless ingenuity of it. Helen and Jamie had fallen silent. When I glanced at them, Jamie was leaning forward, shining the torch on his phone at the lettering on the plaque, trying to decipher it. But Helen was looking at me. When she saw me looking back, she flicked on her usual bland smile, though not before I caught her previous expression – horror, fear, disbelief, a little of all of those.

SHORT STORY THIRD PRIZE

Inner Loop
Josie Turner

It might have been her. I'm almost sure it was her. Why wouldn't it be? She needn't have died, although I've always supposed she did. Same square face, just a little jowly now, with the merry mouth pulled down. Same auburn crop, grown ashy over the years, like a dampened fire. There wouldn't still be freckles. Not in her forties. But the girl holding her hand looked like a freckled daughter—nine, ten maybe.

They were turned back from the flight to London, just as I was, along with the other two hundred passengers thronging the departure lounge. Thousands across the terminal were informed there were no flights into the UK—some network outage, apparently. The Brits were stranded. Locals like me dispersed into hotels, motels, homes. I checked into this bleak roadside room, which looks out on the inner loop linking the freeway to the airport. The sheets smell of disinfectant. The TV remote is sticky. Every morning, I take a cab and circle the inner loop back to the airline's desk, where I'm told 'no dice'. There are shouts and sobs all around me, but I take it calmly. I have shelter. I navigate the encampments of furious sleep-deprived travellers who've spent the last two nights curled like insects on the terminal's floor, waiting for their grounded planes to take flight.

Where is she, the woman with the auburn crop? I haven't seen her again. Perhaps she's given up. Perhaps she had nothing pressing to do in London, so she's returned home with her daughter to their townhouse in the historic quarter. She'll have a fashionable breed of dog, a job in tech, a thriving social media brand. I could look her up online. But I won't. I promised myself long ago I'd never do that.

Or she could be here, in this motel. On the other side of this stippled and flimsy wall. I can hear raised voices and the drone of TVs from every direction. All motels are concrete boxes subdivided into smaller boxes, where sounds bounce around like crazy. Some voices come from years back, dim but unquenchable, especially in the middle of the night. Voices saying things like '*What do you see in Rebecca?*'

*

Headlights strafe the thin curtains. The inner loop is always in use, carrying people through this strange transitory quarter of the city, the place where no-one lives. Out on the strip there's an all-night burger joint, a dry-cleaning kiosk, a tragic bar. Not like the bars of Edward Hopper, curvilinear and gleaming, beautified by melancholy patrons in tobacco-scented nights. It's more like a gas station, a place for people to be hooked up to cheap beer while the minutes of their lives tick past. Who the hell would seek out a bar on the inner loop?

So, I stay in my room and recall the Spaniards Inn. Highgate was miles from where Prav and I lived, but worth the walk most weekends. We could only afford a half-pint each, which we'd drink outside, standing at the barrels, watching the larky British people. They're not buttoned-up at all, the Brits. That's a myth. Before my exchange programme I pictured the guys wearing top hats, the ladies in pastel gloves and hats, like Queen Elizabeth. Londoners came as a shock—so loud and coarse and scruffy, such a multitude of languages and accents. They are rude if they like you, extremely polite if they don't.

She was based in Highgate. I'll say her name, just to myself: Angela. She moved around a lot within that enclave. Always some new rented room in a rambling red-brick villa, always a new crowd of cronies— other exchange students, or interns, or members of a band she liked. I got the feeling she ingratiated herself by always having something to offer—she was a resourceful cook, a fixer of fuses, a planter of seeds, a seller of vintage treasures. Whenever we visited, she would be in another high-ceilinged shabby kitchen, throwing herbs and powders into bubbling saucepans, playing Nirvana on a cassette-machine while people lolled at the long table set in the bay window, rolling joints and waiting to be fed. I never particularly liked her housemates, but they were so transient that it didn't matter. I never particularly liked Angela, and that was more of a problem.

We were both twenty-something postgrads pursuing the same course, living abroad for the first time, thousands of miles from home. We ought to have gelled, but our friendliness was superficial, circumstantial. She was good to me, I must admit, during those first rough months of homesickness. She found street markets and navigated the subway as though she'd lived in London for years. She told me she had nothing back home worth missing. Learning from her, I gradually got the knack of the city. We'd walk through it on summer nights, getting a feel for its secret landmarks, its elegance and squalor.

But I was suspicious of her. And she was contemptuous of me.

Then we met guys. That was the problem right there. Guys.

The crop-haired woman from the airport—let's call her Angela—has a daughter. Which means she did find someone. She always wanted to be attached. She fixated on musicians and actors who crossed our paths, until she met one particular guitarist and went all in. She was crazy about him. Matthew, that was his name. He was an anthropology student who played pub gigs in a not-great band, just when outfits like that were getting signed-up by speculative record companies trying to cash in on Britpop.

Angela was high on it all. She was going to quit her course, apply for British citizenship and make herself indispensable until Matthew married her. I could just picture her in her blue jeans and plaid shirts, cooking in the vast kitchen of some country estate, standing at the hob the way she always did, feet apart, steadying herself like the captain of a ship while red-headed moppets played around her. Matthew would be off on tour.

Maybe that's what happened. Although I've never heard Matthew's name again. And I have reason to believe Angela didn't make it to the English countryside. In fact, I'm pretty certain that she's dead. I should know—I watched her die.

*

Prav was a dental student I met at a university function. So sweetly handsome. His parents had travelled to the UK from India with high expectations for all their sons. At the age of twenty-one Prav had taken the bold step of finding his first girlfriend. He snuggled next to me at various Highgate dinner tables, glancing at Angela's housemates and taking off his glasses to polish their lenses with his shirt tail. Everyone liked Prav. For all his shyness, he could be pretty funny when you got to know him.

Angela liked Prav. She was instinctively indulgent towards all men, and motherly with it. He got the largest portions and the topped-up wine glass. She asked him to look at her teeth, and opened her mouth wide so he could peer inside.

'Very bad,' Prav joshed her. 'I'll pull them out with string if you like.'

'Get lost. I've got American teeth. We've heard of fluoride.'

'Ok, you're blinding me with the dazzle now.'

She flicked him with a dish towel. I was actually charmed by their flirting. I knew how monomaniacal Angela was about Matthew, so her attentions towards Prav were merely a courtesy, in a roundabout way a compliment to me. It didn't happen that evening, the incident that set me on the repetitive inner loop of lifelong rumination. The 'teeth' evening was fun. It happened a few weeks later, at the end of another boozy dinner.

Matthew had joined us for once, and Angela's attention seemed entirely focused on him. Prav and I sat together, but he was drawn into conversation with the guy next to him, and on my other side two girls were giggling together while surreptitiously dividing a pill. So, for quite a long time I was trapped on the long bench, my back to the window, with no one to talk to. Prav kept his hand on my thigh, but I was still alone. Angela sat on Mathhew's lap, facing the window, stroking his neck. I didn't think she even glanced at me. But she must have done. I wonder if something snapped that evening, or if in fact she had always despised me.

As we got drunker, the configuration around the table shifted. The music grew louder. The girls stood up and started dancing, knocking things from the kitchen surfaces. Matthew sloped off to some rendezvous. The guy next to Prav got up to go to the bathroom, and just as he did, before Prav had a chance to turn to me, Angela slid into the vacated spot. I've wondered many times if Angela was motivated by anger at being abandoned by Matthew, even for one evening.

With my back against the windowpane, I watched Angela lean towards Prav, as though to say something confidential. I could see that underneath the table she was tapping his shin with a bare foot. Her toenails were painted orange.

What I heard her say was 'Can you tell me something?'

And sweet Prav said 'Sure.'

'What do you see in Rebecca?'

*

I think what split us up was our overwhelming mutual embarrassment. We never acknowledged that I had overheard the question, and Prav never referred to it. But the question squatted between us like a toad. What, in fact, did he see in me? I was a chunky midwestern girl with nondescript hair in a ponytail. I was homesick, socially awkward, uncertain of myself. And I had a friend who was not a friend. It was this last point which was so damning. Prav was too straightforward, perhaps too young, to grasp that someone could inspire enmity without necessarily deserving it. For someone to ask such a question, there must indeed be something wrong with me.

He didn't have any sisters. That made a difference. He just didn't understand girls.

*

Angela dropped out of our course, to pursue her devotion to Matthew. I didn't meet her again. Our concerned tutor tried to interrogate me, but I said we'd lost touch, which was true. We originated from two different US universities, and there was nothing to connect us. I moped around, survived, met other guys, had fun. My time in London ebbed away. I could have got out unscathed, and if I thought of Angela now it would be with a pinprick of irritation and regret. Because I'd have a different sort of life, a life beyond my own inescapable inner loop.

But I did see her again, by chance. I think I saw her. I think I did. Quite a lot depends on that. Although, looking at it another way, it hardly matters who it was. Only my reaction matters.

*

I was on a train, in the evening. London's outskirts were full of tiny local stations, old and poky, served by trains with only two carriages. Tracks sometimes ran through gullies between streets, so you could look straight into people's sitting rooms and even see the pictures on their walls, and sometimes ran along high embankments, so you could peer down onto gardens and roads. That evening, I was on a high embankment, and the train was dawdling in one of these parochial stations. I was drowsing over a free paper. My flight home was a couple of days away.

I glanced across the empty platform and down onto a narrow approach path. I couldn't see much, what with the dusk, the fencing and the obscuring weeds. There was a lot of overgrowth and trash, and the path was unlit. But I could make out a girl's head bobbing up the steep incline. She had a cap of auburn hair, and Angela's jaunty gait. A plaited leather strap was visible over her shoulder, just like the strap of Angela's book bag. She might have been wearing a plaid shirt. But I just don't know. I have reconstructed the moment so often in my mind that the image is furred and blurry.

I saw two guys approach from behind and jump her. She folded immediately, just dropped straight down below my line of vision. The guys seemed to feast on her, raising their fists and driving them downwards in silence.

The train's door stood open. The seconds oozed by. Then there came the electronic ticking warning of closing doors, and then they swooshed shut. It all seemed to take a while. And in that time, I did nothing.

I looked around at a few other passengers, who were chatting to one another, or reading, or dozing. It must have been a weekend. No crowds, no hurry. No one else saw.

I stood up, too late, and moved towards the doors. The train slid forward and picked up speed. No one had a cell phone in those days. I thought, just what the hell should I do?

I thought, '*What do you see in Rebecca?*'
And I sat back down.

*

I never heard Angela's name mentioned again. I resumed my life in the States and found a diplomatic job in DC as planned. Got married, divorced—the usual. I wondered all the time what anyone saw in me.

I saw the girl folding, over and over again.

On the inner loop of my conscience, I've passed the same milestones every day—the evening light, the electronic ticking sound, standing up, sitting down. Nirvana. Orange-painted toenails and a slender arched foot—decades ago, far away.

*

I have put off this trip to London so many times, but my department was insistent. I thought it would be ok.

I'm only supposed to pass through London on my way to Cheltenham. I can white-knuckle a few train rides, I guess.

Flights are back on. I checked out of the motel, took my last cab along the inner loop. My thoughts are quieter in daylight. People get mugged: I got mugged in Chicago one New Year's Eve. Shit happens. I'm not responsible for every act of violence in the world.

She's ahead of me in the queue at the gate. Cropped hair, green dress. A little heavier these days, but still with the capable sea-captain stance. She looks like a woman who can cook, plant a garden, run a business. The girl holds her hand, bobs at her side.

I would like to walk ahead and tap this woman on the shoulder. I'd like to start again, free myself, get off the loop. If I call 'Angela?' and she turns around, then I'll know. If she looks at me, I'll remember her eyes.

All Business
James Watson

She had him pinned against the front door of the apartment, her eyes so close to his he found it difficult to focus. Her shoulders heaved with each breath.

'It will work. I promise you,' he mumbled, finding it difficult to convince even himself.

She did not let up. She had him by the lapels of his short raincoat and the chains and locks of the sturdy door were pressing painfully into his back.

'I need you to do this, Matty.'

'That's enough, Liebling.'

But he had to shift his weight forward and take her wrists until he had re-established his balance and was holding her away from him. She started to cry.

'She's helped others. There's no reason she won't help us,' he tried.

The woman broke away and retreated into the dimly lit kitchen where he found her holding onto the counter with the back of her other hand against her mouth. He cradled her from behind and whispered calming words to her until she straightened and, with a forced attempt at vigor, made a show of appraising his appearance.

There was little that could be done at this stage about the sag of Matty's pants at the knee, or the stitching of his left shoe but she set about to straighten his coat.

'Oh, there's a mark around the pocket!' she said.

She wetted a cloth and applied it earnestly.

'I should go.'

'Confidence! Remember, she's only a person, like us.'

'I know.'

'Tell me again.'

'Tradition. Community. Consecration.'

'Don't forget the consecration. All the souls, they are the most important.'

She brushed his coat straight one more time with a slap of her hand.

He leant forward to kiss her, but she moved away.

'The gift,' she said.

He tapped his chest pocket. 'I have it.'

The bus stop was only a few blocks from the apartment, but he arrived only just in time for the early evening bus that was headed for the heart of Manhattan, and he found a seat towards the middle. From Queens it was almost an hour's ride, and he produced a small novel from his coat pocket that he had set aside for just such a period of solitude as this. However, his mind could not hold on to the words on the page and, after reading over the same paragraphs a number of times, he slipped the slim volume back into his pocket.

'Culture. Communication. Congregation.' His mind was playing tricks with him. He had nothing to divert it with.

At Jay Street a homeless man managed to slip past the driver and began working the passengers for money.

'You, Friend,' the man said locking eyes with Matty from some distance away. The tramp progressed rapidly up the length of the bus towards him, as Matty hurriedly fumbled for his novel. Before he could work it out of his pocket the man was beside him in a suffocating funk of his own odor. Matty shrank into the chair, glancing around for signs of assistance but all eyes were quickly averted.

'For food, for the desolate and afflicted. Be generous, Friend.'

A filthy tattooed hand stretched out towards him.

Matty sensed his fellow passengers were closely following the exchange. He swallowed, not knowing how he should respond. He should help this man. Yes, of course, he must, and he considered whether he should reach for change or extract a larger sum from the wallet in his jacket. Which was the right thing?

The hand twitched, urging a decision.

'That's quite enough of that, Pal.'

The driver had left the cab, and he yanked the man backwards and propelled him to the doors, thrusting him out into the darkness of the early evening.

'My enemies are many,' the man cried as he disappeared from view.

Matty's sense of relief that the decision was taken from him was clouded by a foreboding that he had been tested and failed. Had the man been quoting the psalms?'

He got off at the bottom of Central Park and walked the rest of the way to 87th Upper West Side.

It was one of the old-style apartment buildings, discreet but wealthy looking. He was made to wait in the lobby whilst everything was cleared with the resident concerned, then he was walked by the receptionist to a specific elevator that would take him directly to the lady's apartment. He would be met on arrival at the 5th floor.

It was a young woman who stood opposite the opening doors of the elevator. She did not attempt to take his hand but asked for his coat, which she expertly wrapped around a clothes hanger and placed in a concealed cupboard.

'Mrs Collins will give you 15 minutes.' The woman was still in her twenties, he suspected. She spoke slightly faster than Matty was used to and, although she had her full attention on him, he felt as though he could step to one side, and she wouldn't notice. Her foundation makeup had been applied flawlessly across her young face and the lines of her lipstick and eyeliner were more precisely drawn than her own features that God had given her.

'Please respect her age, she isn't to be shocked, and you should not raise your voice with her. If she tires, you should make your excuses and leave.'

The young woman's face glowed in the low orange light of the apartment entrance. Her cultured voice bounced across the marbled walls and floor and round the marbled heads of the family forebears that stood on plinths, but Matty was not listening to what she was saying.

'Tradition.' he rehearsed. 'Community.'

'This way. Mrs Collins said she will see you in her private withdrawing room.'

The personal assistant leant to the large brass handles of double doors, allowed him to pass her, and then withdrew, closing the doors with an almost imperceptible click behind him.

He was temporarily overwhelmed. The walls were painted a uniform white under lighting that was so bright he almost had to shield his eyes. With the exception of a single enormous painting, there was no other decor on the walls at all. The painting itself dominated the central wall. A woman stood on broken ground, huge industrial earth movers in the rear, a hard hat cradled in front of her. The aggressive intensity of the woman's stare spoke of the power of the Collins' business. She was the developer of the cityscape that had made her family both famous and wealthy.

'Do you approve?'

An old woman was observing him from an antique chair. She could not be anyone other than the same woman, only 50 years older. The angle of the old woman's head and the piercing blue eyes were identical to the image he had been studying. He had made a mistake coming here.

'I always wonder why he painted in the Empire State but not the Chrysler. Quite curious don't you think?'

Matty had not noticed the cityscape in the distance.

'You're a priest, Mr Kurtz?'

'It is a slight misunderstanding.'

'You're not? Your introduction informed me you were trying to save your church. Perhaps you could elucidate why you're here.' She motioned for him to sit.

Matty lowered himself into a delicate looking chair some ten yards away from Mrs Collins.

'It's a church in Queens, the Lutheran church near…'

'You'll have to speak up. My hearing is terrible with this cold weather. It will be the snow next. I hate the onset of winter.'

'Your Son-in-Law is redeveloping the area around Sackton. He's obtained permission to level the entire area and put new apartment blocks and shops on it. We'll be obliged to sell the church to him, and it will be demolished. The traditions of the area will be lost and the history that is invested in the church, dating back over 200 years, with some of the first German immigrants…'

She held up her hand. He stopped.

'Why are you here? If you're not the priest?'

'This is my church, my congregation.' Not congregation, he cursed himself. That was the wrong word. 'I am training to be a lay preacher and

I have been active in this church community for over ten years. It's a living, worshiping community, unlike many other churches in New York.'

'Is it a pretty church?'

Matty took a deep breath. He had already skipped ahead and the subjective beauty of the building was an unnecessary diversion. 'It's a church with a lot of history. Much of the tradition of the area is invested in that building, those who have lived and died in the area. There are some famous New York names associated with it.'

'So, it's not.'

Matty was aware of the painting out the corner of his eye, and he wished it wasn't there. He wasn't sure where to go now. It had seemed so simple when Anna had written it out for him.

'Mr Kurtz?'

'It may not have the same beauty as some of the Catholic churches or even the Nazarene churches, but Lutherans are not focused on such things. Even so, it is considered an important landmark in its own right.'

The old lady considered him carefully. 'Buildings come, buildings go.' She waved her hand dismissively. 'It's how cities progress. We keep the very special ones, but few buildings earn the right to remain in perpetuity. What makes you so invested in an ugly church? Why do you really want me to intercede with my son-in-law? We can put life into buildings, but they have no souls of their own.'

'It's a church.'

'Henry VIII pulled down thousands of monasteries in England. In part due to the influence of Luther himself, by the way. A church has no more right to be kept than a Walmart store, especially nowadays. No one needs churches, we've moved on from rising damp and colicky vicars. If there is a God, people have chosen not to meet him in ancient tombs, not to be restricted by real estate. not to replicate the paradigms of the past. Luther would have approved, would he not? Luther the democratising force of the Christian religion, fracturing the intermediation of the Catholic clergy?

'Community,' Matty said, desperately.

'What about it?'

'There is a very strong Lutheran community in the area and the church is the centre, the only centre for our community. There are…'

A young boy, of around ten years old, entered the room interrupting the uncertain flow of the German, as he spoke. The child wore red and white patterned pyjamas and his thick, youthful hair shone brilliantly under the stark lighting.

'This is my Grandson, Mr Kurtz. Say hello to our guest, Gabriel.'

'Good evening, Sir.'

Mr Kurtz is here to stop your father from developing a part of Queens. Do you think he'll have much success?'

The boy shook his head. 'I don't think it's likely.'

'Tell Mr Kurtz why that is.'

'Father's all business, Grandma.'

The old woman smiled. 'Yes, he's all business.' She had the boy around the waist in a very firm grasp, pulling him too strongly against the side of her armchair, but he did not complain. This was, perhaps, an often-repeated scene.

'Before you go to bed you can entertain us at the piano. Do you have a piece you've practised?'

The boy broke free of her grip and walked over to a small upright piano that Matty had not noticed. He sat on the stool and began, hesitantly at first, to play a simple piece which Matty recognized; a German folk song Matty had been taught by his mother. The boy began to sing the words of the familiar song, in a high, innocent voice. The boy's straight back moved and gyrated under the demands of the music until finally, he stopped. He gently replaced the lid over the keys and returned to kiss his grandmother goodnight, leaving as quickly as he had come.

'Do you have children, Mr Kurtz?'

He was momentarily thrown by the question. He had been thinking about the boy and the song and the memory of his mother.

'I...No, we have no children,' he managed. 'You are very blessed.'

The old lady stirred in her seat. It seemed, from her expression, she had tired of him.

'I will speak with Gabriel's father, but I can't promise anything.' She rose slowly. 'I must have my dinner now, otherwise my staff will be upset with me, but I will walk with you to the elevator.'

She had a cane, and, when she came alongside Matty, she took his arm and the two of them walked awkwardly together. When they reached the withdrawing room doors Matty leant down to open them and spoke the part he had not wanted to raise.

'There's a consecrated graveyard at the back of the Church,' Matty said. They proceeded into the dim entrance hall amongst the busts of the Collins family ancestors.

'That would all be taken care of. My son-in-law does not cut corners with that sort of detail. Deconsecration, removal of remains, he's an old hand at that sort of thing.' A pause. 'Or is that not what you meant?'

Matty opened the cupboard and slipped on his coat.

'We had a baby girl. Olive.'

Mrs Collins tapped her cane distractedly.

'And your girl? She's buried in this graveyard?'

'She lived for two weeks. There was a complication with the birth, she never opened her eyes. We buried her next to a lilac tree in the lee of the church last year. My wife…we both fear to lose her again.'

The woman pressed the button to call the elevator and it opened smoothly in front of them.

'I almost forgot.' Matty reached into an inside pocket and produced a thin package, which he passed to Mrs Collins. 'A small gift, from me and my wife. I am sorry for taking your time. My wife believed in you.'

The old woman held the elevator door with her cane and Matty stepped in. She nodded her head towards him then withdrew the cane.

When the elevator doors had closed, she tucked the stick under her arm and unpicked the wrapping of the gift. It was the work of a woman, very precise and pleasingly folded. Mrs Collins picked out from the decorative paper a wooden frame for a photograph, hand-made with a simple but elegant inlay.

She retreated into her room and placed it on the piano. Though it seemed plain against the seasoned mahogany of the Steinbach, a bright photograph, of Gabriel perhaps, could bring out the beauty in its simplicity.

A dying breed
Tony Durrant

The camera bag and daypack lay in the corner where he had thrown them. Harry eyed them from the bed and raised the vodka bottle in a silent toast. He swigged, felt the warm fingers of the spirit then watched his cigarette smoke as it dispersed in the draught from the ceiling fan. The muezzin started, the wailing prayer strong enough to carry above the cacophony of the street below the hotel window. Harry stood uncertainly, stooped to the bags and carried them to the bed. His hand trembled as he fumbled with the straps of the camera bag. Some of the lenses were cracked. There was a scratched camera body and a dog-eared notebook.

He took another mouthful of vodka then upended the daypack. Shirt, towel, water bottle, two packets of cigarettes, toothbrush and paste in a plastic bag. The side pocket held a press ID card and a wallet. The brown leather of the wallet was worn dark and smooth on the edges. Harry imagined it lying in the warmth of James' pocket.

He pulled a photo from the wallet. There they were, standing by a Toyota pick-up, wearing obligatory sunglasses. James had his arm around his shoulder. In the pick-up, militia men with AK47s made victory signs with their fingers. There was another photo in the wallet: a smiling woman wrapped in a summer dress, standing on a lawn. Her hair glowed in the sunlight as it fell to her shoulders. Harry put both photos in his shirt pocket and pulled a credit card from the wallet. He ran a finger over the lettering: Mr James Bedford.

Harry raised the bottle. 'Well, James. It looks like you're paying for your last trip home.'

*

The cluster of people started to disperse from around the grave. Harry had stood on the fringes and retired to the shade of an ancient yew. He watched the vicar take James' mother by the arm and steer her along the narrow churchyard path. The young woman from the photo was talking to the undertaker who scanned the mourners and nodded towards Harry. She held up her long skirt with one hand and strode between the headstones towards him. Harry watched as a blonde tendril escaped from beneath her hat. It bounced as she walked. She extended her hand.

'Sophie Bedford. You must be Harry. Thanks for bringing him home.'

'Oh, hi. It was the least I could do. He was...we were friends.'

'I know. He wrote about you.'

Harry was in the process of lighting a cigarette and held out his packet.

She peered at them then took one. He held out his lighter. His hand trembled.

She swept her skirt beneath her and sat, crossing her legs. She inhaled, stifled a cough and threw her head back to blow smoke into the air.

'Christ, what a mess. Poor bloody James. My baby brother finally home, lying shoulder to shoulder with the other Bedfords. There they are...boys who never grew up. Oh, we managed to produce the occasional cleric and there's even an academic over there.' She waved her hand towards the graves. He noticed a pale wrist and scarlet fingernails. 'The rest? Action men through and through and in the finest traditions of the Bedfords the broken-hearted women weep over the freshly turned earth of our little piece of England. His old regiment wanted to send some chaps in uniform and a flag for the coffin. I think Mother swore at some senior officer over the phone. We haven't heard from them since.'

She turned her head and Harry felt her gaze. 'And you, Harry? Where will your bones lie?'

'Missouri...I guess.'

She opened her mouth then changed her mind.

'Thanks again for bringing him home. We're in your debt.'

She dropped the cigarette and stepped on it. As she rose Harry stood with her. 'I have...Sophie, I have a confession.'

She arched an eyebrow. 'Do go on.'

'I'm not in your debt. He…I mean James. He paid for this…I used his credit card to fly him back.'

Her eyes widened. From that moment Harry would always describe them as cornflower blue. She put a hand over her mouth to stifle a laugh. 'Well, I never. You old rogue. Wait till I tell Mother. What a hoot.'

'No, please, Sophie. Of all people, please don't tell Mrs…your mother. It's just that. We were broke, I was broke and, well, it was an easy fix. Out there…you know, people turn a blind eye.'

She placed a finger over her lips. 'Don't worry Harry. Your secret is safe with me. I don't mind at all. James certainly won't.'

She laughed again and shook her head. 'Listen, I'd love to stand and chat but there are guests to take care of. James' old friends from that awful public school of his will want watering so we're having drinks in the White Horse, just along the lane. And you must come and meet Mother. She'll also want to thank you. And your cigarettes would be very welcome.'

She smiled and Harry's gaze wandered from the cornflower blue to the laughter lines by her eyes. She strode back through the graves, a hand on her hat.

*

He ducked through the low door of the pub and followed the sound of chatter. It led him to a side bar where the older relatives were toying with sherry and tea. James' mother was seated, talking with the vicar. Sophie was standing by the window with an elderly man. She had taken off her hat and unpinned her hair, which bounced on her shoulders as she moved her head.

Harry walked to the bar to buy a drink, nodding at the relatives who caught his eye as he waited. The room was hung with horse brasses and crossed with ancient beams. Some of the guests were threading through a side door to a garden which he could see through the leaded windows. He took his drink and stooped through the door onto a path circling a lawn dotted with tables and surrounded by trees and shrubs. James' peers had taken over a large table which was cluttered with glasses and champagne bottles. Three children were running around on the grass in bare feet, shrieking in excitement.

He found a wooden seat in the shade, the arms furred with lichen. He drained his glass and fished in an inside pocket for his hip flask to refill it. As he returned the flask, he felt the photos and pulled one of them out. As he held it he saw that his hand had stopped shaking. It was the image of him and James with the militiamen in the pick-up. A shadow passed over him. Her skirt rustled as she sat.

She nodded at the photo. 'May I?'

Harry hesitated then passed it to her.

She tutted. 'Guns, bombs, boys…'

She passed it back and pushed a lock of hair from her forehead with a red fingernail. 'Mother and I were so pleased when he came back from Afghanistan…unscathed. Well, when I say unscathed, it had changed him. He had an edge. Drank more. When he left the army, we breathed a sigh of relief, hoped he'd had his fill. But no, not dear James. He's… he was, a Bedford, after all. Afghanistan was only the start. I can see him now, whisky in hand, waffling on about photojournalism and 'finding his calling'.'

She shielded her eyes and looked towards the top boughs of an ancient elm where a wood pigeon was calling, undisturbed by the children. She sipped her drink and smiled at the children's antics.

Harry studied the down on the side of her neck, saw the lines again by her eyes. He recognised the description of her brother. He had heard it before, how on leaving the army James had taken a crash course in photography and bought a plane ticket to Iraq. Then Ukraine and Syria, where they met. James was enthusiastic but also had an eye, won some awards. Typical James, thought Harry.

'Mother would worry about him. She would be glued to the news. I would invent emails from him to ease her worry.' She turned and put her hand on his arm. 'Come on Harry. I'm a big girl. How did it happen?'

Harry looked at his empty glass. 'I need another drink. Would you like one?'

He tried to stand but she held him back by the arm. 'Don't try to avoid the bloody question, Harry. What happened?' She took a breath and lowered her voice. 'Harry. Please…the Foreign and Commonwealth Office mentioned an explosion and insisted that was all they knew.'

He sat back and fumbled for his cigarettes. His hands were shaking again. He felt Sophie staring at him, willing him to answer. They were interrupted by a woman's voice.

'Hi, Soph. Sorry to interrupt but I hear your friend here was with James…that he's also a photographer?'

Harry stood and extended a hand. 'Yeah…we were buddies.'

She took his hand. 'Oh, that's sweet. Sorry to bother you but we were wondering if you could do the honours…you being a professional and all.' She motioned towards the crowd around the large table. 'A photo? It's just that the old gang aren't often together these days.'

Harry tried to sit back down. 'No, I'm afraid…I'd…'

The woman kept hold of Harry's hand and held her phone out in front of him. Harry looked at Sophie for help, but she stood and shrugged. 'I'm off to the bar. Good luck.'

The woman gently pulled his arm. 'Come on, Harry. You'll make a much better job of it than any of us.' She steered him across the lawn. 'Hey everybody, this is Harry. He's going to take a photograph.'

There was a murmur of approval which he acknowledged with a wave of his hand. The woman flapped a hand at him. 'Come on, Harry, you're the expert. How would you like us?'

Harry glanced at the sun and took a few sidesteps. He inhaled to steady his breathing. 'Ok. Let's see. Look this way.'

He could see the grinning faces in the screen, glasses held aloft, practised smiles. 'Take a few, Harry. Cheese!' Their laughter started to echo. The image shook and he glimpsed James' face in the phone's screen. He blinked and stared at the screen. His vision blurred. He felt himself staggering. Falling.

*

She was wearing a white cotton dress and a straw hat. It was the one she was wearing in the photo he had found in James' wallet. Her calves were tanned. The air was warm, insects buzzed in the hedgerow.

She smiled over her shoulder. 'She likes you. You charmed her. I never thought you had it in you.'

'Ha, ha. Your mother is a lovely lady. She's how I imagined her.'

She stopped by a gate which led through the hedgerow. 'So, he talked about her? Us?'

'Yes…of course. A lot.' The path wound through a hay meadow on the side of the hill. He could see the tower of the church below where James was buried.

Harry raised his hand towards the landscape. 'He loved this place. He spoke of it often. I can see why. I've been to England before but only to London. This place is…it's special.'

There was a weather-beaten wooden bench by the footpath. She sat and took off her hat, swept her hair off her forehead.

He sat by her. 'Yes, he spoke about this place, about you and your mother. There are times, in those places, when home and kin are all that matter. They are the anchor among the chaos.'

Sophie nodded. He stared at the horizon and could feel her looking at him, but he kept his gaze fixed on the view; the rippling of the wheat in the wind in the field below them, a kestrel hovering over a meadow on the far side of the valley.

'So, who did you talk about, Harry? Who's your anchor?'

He felt for his cigarettes and offered her one. She shook her head.

'You've got to give those up. They're bloody awful.'

'Maybe. One day.'

'The other day…at the pub…What was it?'

'Jet lag, apparently, according to the doc.'

She shook her head. 'It was more than that, Harry. You went somewhere. You were out for hours.'

He stood up and took a step so that he had his back to her.

'He adored you, Sophie. Never stopped talking about you. You were his anchor.'

'Tell me…What happened?'

'It was getting late. We knew we'd pushed it. Had some great shots. The sun…well, at that time of day over there it gives that special light. There's a glow…it's the dust. Ahmed, our minder, he wasn't happy. We had to get back to the district where the hotel was. It wasn't safe in darkness for us. Bullets by day, kidnappers by night. There was some open ground between ruined houses. A short cut. Ahmed wasn't sure about it. James…Well, you know, always out front.'

He drew on his cigarette and looked up at the clouds. 'I thought he had tripped at first. I didn't take it in. Such a small bang. More of a crack really. An IED. A small one. There was a lot of blood… his leg. He lay there and swore. He looked at me, he looked at me and he grinned through the pain. That boyish grin… made some joke about not playing cricket again. Ahmed wouldn't let me go to him, said there would be others. He was right. There always is. Was. Ahmed phoned for help. It took too long.'

Across the valley, the kestrel swooped. A dog barked and a tractor revved as it climbed the hill out of the village.

She stood and put her arm on his shoulder. 'So…and?'

'He bled. His last words were, 'it's time I went home'. Then he lost consciousness, he bled… He felt no pain. He was in shock.'

'There was nothing? Nothing you could do?'

'What could I do? I…' He took a breath. 'I took photographs.'

He could hear her crying; small sobs, like a wounded animal.

'I took photographs. It's what I do. Did.'

Harry knew he would never take another photograph as long as he lived but this was not the time to tell her. The sorrow had passed to her and it was her time to grieve. He turned. She was sitting with her head in her hands. Her hat had fallen onto the grass below the bench, its ribbon ruffled by the summer breeze.

Hide
Chris Belson

Every Saturday, before the sun had come up and the droves of dog walkers and families had begun to break the silence of the morning, Patrick would slip unseen through the empty woods and dirt tracks of the country park to a little bird-hide by the edge of the lake at its centre.

To anyone who happened to be passing by, he would be barely visible. A brief wake of movement in a tree line, a flash of faded khaki sliding between two willows, a fleeting shadow caught in the still, black surface of the water. Then he'd be gone, safely inside the secret womb of the stilted, wooden hide by the lake. Here, for just a few hours each week, he felt as though he were the only human left in the world. In fact, sometimes he didn't feel human at all. Inside that little hut, when the world was still sleeping, he almost felt as though he had transcended form altogether. He was just a spirit, the morning itself, watching life unfold around him, and that's how he liked it.

Today, just as he had done so many times before, Patrick sat alone on the bench in the hide. He unhooked the latches and lifted the shutter from the window, watched the cold, pre-dawn light catch in the ripples of the lake, and the dew on the reeds, and in his own breath, as it rolled out and dissolved into the air around him. Then he closed his eyes and listened for the sun to rise.

At first, it was just a blackbird, and then a robin, and then a thrush. Woodpigeon. Wren. Sedge warbler. Chiffchaff. Blackcap. Patrick picked each of them out, one by one, until they simply rolled together into a jumbled, wash of song. And beneath that, almost hidden under the birdsong, the sound of beetles stirring, of the beating wings of flies above the lake, of tree branches yawning in the warming light, of leaves unfurling. Patrick bathed in it all, as if tuning into a secret frequency, witness to the slow bloom of dawn, like a curtain being lifted. Then suddenly, the moment was broken by the sound of a board creaking behind him. He sat motionless for a moment, as a deer might at the sound of a branch breaking on the forest floor. He opened his eyes and was, for a moment, blinded by daybreak. He blinked and rubbed them until the soft, bleary forms of the park and the hide swirled back into focus and found that he was no longer alone. He turned to see a young woman, standing at the entrance of the hide.

'Thought I'd be the only one here, this early,' she said, smiling.

For a moment Patrick didn't speak. He just looked up at her, dumbfounded, as if she were an apparition, or an echo of some strange dream.

'Hope I haven't scared off any birds?' Her voice was loud, so different to the soft, babbling sounds outside that Patrick felt himself jump slightly when she spoke. In his mind, he saw the little warblers and finches scattering from their branches. In fact, for a brief moment he thought that he might even have felt the sun itself retreat back behind the horizon at the sound of her words.

'No…' he said. 'No, I haven't…' He looked to his binoculars, still capped on the sill of the window in front of him, and for a second, he kept looking at them, their eyes closed, just as his own had been, moments before.

The woman came further into the hide and bent down next to Patrick to look out across the lake. She was carrying a towel that was rolled into a tight, white scroll beneath her arm. He could feel the warmth of her body next to his and for an instant, felt himself leaning in towards her. Before he realised what he was doing, she turned and spoke to him again.

'Look at us two, up with the larks!'

'Sorry?'

'You know, *up with the larks*?'

'You don't really get larks…not around here.' Patrick said quietly. 'Skylarks, maybe, but only further out in the farmland or heath…'

The woman looked at Patrick, smiling vacantly, but then turned again to the window. Steam rose from the night-damp timber of the hut as it warmed by the sunlight. The sound of the birds had risen now too, into an overtone of lively chatter. It seemed to bubble and echo around them, underscoring their own silence.

'Why do birds sing in the morning?' the woman asked. 'What do you think they're saying to each other?'

Patrick thought about this for a moment. He'd never considered what they might be saying to one another, as if they spoke in a language that we could understand. As they listened, Patrick thought that perhaps he could make out the odd conversation between birds, after all. A call and response. A canon of exchanges. 'I'm here! I'm here!' one would say. 'I hear you, but where? I hear you, but where?' the other would reply.

'Oh, I wouldn't know about that...' he said to the woman. 'Are they not just singing because it's morning?'

'Yes, maybe you're right. That could be it,' she replied.

Patrick looked sideways at the woman. She must have been about twenty years younger than him. She was wearing an old, out of shape tracksuit and a puffer jacket, and smelt of sleep, as if she'd just rolled out of bed and wandered outside. He could almost still see the creases in her cheek, from where a pillow might have pressed against her as she slept.

'Isn't it strange?' she said, 'They're all tweeting their little hearts out, but you can't see them. It's like we're just listening to one of those CDs you buy at garden centres. May I?'

The woman gestured towards Patrick's binoculars but had already reached across to pick them up before he could nod politely in consent. She lifted them to her eyes and then immediately laughed.

'Lens caps.' she said, as she slid the caps from their places.

Patrick watched as she blindly fumbled around to find the focus wheel, awkwardly wrestling with the eyepieces, as she folded and unfolded the bridge to try and fit her eyes. Finally, she settled them against her face and began to scan wildly across the landscape.

'It must be exciting to see a kingfisher, or something really exotic? A lesser-spotted flame-crest, or something like that?'

There was no such bird. Did she know that? Only a lesser-spotted woodpecker, or a firecrest. Neither of which he'd ever seen here.

'Kingfishers are such beautiful birds, don't you think?' she continued.

Patrick wanted to tell her that the most exciting birds, the ones he most desperately wanted to spot, were almost always small, and brown, and seemingly unremarkable in appearance. The vivid, brightly coloured birds, with shocks of electric feathers, and frills, and crests on fire, paled in comparison to those scarce, shy species that he loved. The ones who knew how to disappear into the restless pattern of the world around them. The ones you might pass by in the leaf-litter, without knowing how close you were to something so beautiful.

'Yes. You'll sometimes see a kingfisher, if you're lucky.' he replied.

The woman placed the binoculars back on the sill, then sighed deeply.

'Well, I'm probably disturbing you.' she said, 'Thanks for letting me have a look.'

And with that, before Patrick could even reply, she had strolled out of the hide, and he was on his own again. She had gone so suddenly, that Patrick momentarily questioned whether she had been there at all.

He leaned over to his binoculars. Slowly placed the cups to his eyes, tentatively, as if looking into the unknown, as if someone else's gaze might now be burnt into the lens' grain, but it was just the lake. Only the lake, and the park, and the sun slowly breaking through the stirring trees. He watched as the coots and moorhens began to drift out around the water's edge, weaving through the rushes and under the twisted roots that forked like fingers into the shallows. Steam was rising thinly now, hanging on the skin of the lake as if it were sweating. The trees too, were beginning to move, their shadows trembling with an almost invisible motion. The spring of a branch. The flash of something across a copse. Silhouettes agitated with waking life. Then he saw the woman. Just a hazy figure in the fringes of his view at first, but then her full form, emerging from the vegetation. He pulled her into focus and watched as she carefully descended a little bank on the far side, to a small, flat shore at the water's edge. There, she hung her towel on the arm of a nearby birch and started to undress.

For a moment, Patrick lowered the binoculars and turned away, but then felt himself slowly drawn back to the scene. He watched, full of shame, as she first stripped off her sweater, and then her t-shirt and her trousers, until finally, she was down to just a swimming costume that she must have been wearing underneath, all this time. Through the binoculars, she was close enough for Patrick to see the goose-pimpled skin of her legs and arms, as she stretched and bent her body in the chilled air. Slowly, she edged forward and then began to wade out, breaking the still lake's mirror with each step, until it was gently lapping around her ankles, and then her knees, and then her waist, before finally, she reached out her arms and launched herself into the cold water. In an instant she had woken the silent, dark glass of its surface into a wake of movement, her pale figure, cutting across it like a swan.

Surely, she must know that I can see her, Patrick thought. After all, she herself had looked out at this same view only minutes ago. As Patrick watched, he imagined all of the wildlife around them, watching too. The birds in their branches, voles in the cleft of a bank, squirrels from the openings of their dreys. A thousand bead-like eyes, peering down at the pool, watching this strange woman as she swam.

He could still smell her in the hide. Her soft perfume hung in the air where she had stood, so different to that of the damp earth and wood that it seemed to overwhelm him, as if it were he that was swimming in her. Outside, her distant, pale, figure continued to glide towards the centre, carving a steady line across to the middle of the lake. Then, without warning, she rose up into an arc and rolled her body over into the water, diving head-first beneath the surface. Patrick watched as her legs followed and slipped into the lake, until she had disappeared completely. Just like a duck might, or a grebe, swimming down to the bottom to feed, before popping back up a metre or so from where it had vanished.

Patrick waited and began to scan the lake to catch sight of her bursting out of the water again, but she didn't come up. In the unbearable silence that followed, he found himself counting the seconds under his breath, desperately searching for a shadow, or boil of water, to announce that she was about to resurface, but nothing came. Before he knew what he was doing, he found himself stumbling down the slope that led to the bank by the hide, slipping as the clay gave way under his feet. Then he too was in the water, pitching, heron-like through the silt, until he was knee deep and couldn't go out any further. For a moment he bent down, about to heave himself into the water, but then rose again in defeat, as if seeing his face reflected on its surface and reeling back in horror. The sun was above the trees now and had turned the quiet pond into a shimmering, golden foil. The chorus of birds had petered out into a broken coda of whispers and trills and Patrick closed his eyes again and listened, searching for those voices in the trees, until they were all he could hear.

Home Turf
Joy Clews

'Those sparrows have no shame. Just look at 'em carrying on,' George says, jerking his chin in the direction of the fence. He shakes his head but continues to watch them avidly. Enviously, perhaps. The female's perched on the fence with the male balanced on top of her like they're a pair of circus acrobats. They'd be better off on the grass. Why make life harder than it needs to be?

'He's got stamina, I'll give him that,' I say.

'Exhibitionist,' George grunts in reply. He puts the two mugs he's carrying on the patio table and slumps onto the chair next to me, blowing his breath out noisily as though the act of sitting down is hard work. I glance at him.

'Old bones,' he offers as explanation, his eyes back on the sparrows.

I don't reply. His bones are seven months younger than mine.

'They're not the best looking of birds,' he says.

'They can't help that. It's not like they have any choice in the matter.'

'Monogamous though.'

'How do you know?'

He wraps his hands around his mug and blows on his tea, something he always does, even if it's been poured long enough for it to have gone cold.

He shrugs.

'Can't remember. I probably heard it on a nature programme on the telly.' He takes a gulp of his drink. 'With a bit of luck they'll nest in the bush by the shed again, then we'll see the young when they fledge.'

I nod without enthusiasm.

The pressure washer, a variety of attachments and a large container of cleaning fluid are lined up at the edge of the small, paved area where we are sitting. We call it the patio, although when George laid the crazy paving slabs more than forty years ago no one around here used that word. He follows my gaze.

'I thought I'd spruce it up a bit this afternoon.'

It doesn't need cleaning in my view, but I say nothing. It's best if he keeps busy.

*

When I've drained my mug George clears away the lunch things and I head to the greenhouse. It's a place of warmth and shelter for me as well as the tomatoes. I inhale the sweetness of them as I move methodically from plant to plant pinching out the side shoots. It keeps my fingers occupied and kills a bit of time.

I look up when I hear footsteps clumping along the garden path. George is carrying something in his palm. As he passes the open door, he unfurls his fingers to show me.

'Young goldfinch,' he says.

The bird looks tiny and delicate against his large, gnarled hand. Its feathers are grey, not having had time to change into the bright red and yellow plumage of adulthood.

'Looks like a cat's had it,' he says, before continuing to the end of the garden. When he reaches the compost heap, he continues to cradle the dead bird in one hand while he picks up a trowel with the other and digs a hole in the ground by the supporting wooden panel. He gently places the goldfinch in it before filling the space with soil and patting it down.

On his way back he stops suddenly and looks at me. I don't realise I'm crying until I feel the tears running down my cheeks.

'Come here,' he says, opening his arms.

He makes shushing noises as he strokes my hair. I lean against him and breathe in the earthy smell of his padded gardening shirt as I try to focus on the slow, steady beating of his heart.

'It just got to me,' I tell him when my sobbing subsides.

'I know, love.' He's stopped telling me it will be alright. We both know it isn't true.

He pulls a crumpled tissue out of his pocket and a flurry of white flakes float like snow to the ground.

'Here,' he says gently, holding the tissue close to my face. 'Wipe your eyes and give your nose a blow.'

He kisses the top of my head then steps away and draws the backs of his hands across his eyes.

'Just listen to that lot,' he says, looking beyond the doorway of the greenhouse.

'What?'

'The sparrows, cheeping and chattering away. Life goes on, so they say.'

He sighs. I don't say anything. I don't need to – he knows my views about life going on.

*

I wait until I can hear the drone of the pressure washer before I go to the vegetable patch. It's small but there's sufficient space to grow a few favourites—potatoes, carrots, and broad beans. The beans are leaning in towards the carrots as though they're sharing secrets with them. I'll tie them to the canes later; for now, I hold them back with my arm so I can see between the neat rows of vegetables. The footprint is there, just as it has been for the last 386 days. It's long and broad, formed by the sole of a hefty hiking boot. Looking at it, most people would think it belonged to a man. Emma always had big feet, even as a baby. The last time she visited she came into the garden to help me to put the canes in the ground. I was irritated by the way she clomped around the carefully prepared soil. Now I'm grateful that she did.

I feel closest to her when I'm here. It's best in the winter when the tread pattern is stiff with frost. Cold, dry weather makes it less precarious. Whenever rain is forecast, I protect it using a frame made from pieces of cane and some tarpaulin from Emma's camping days. George made the frame soon after it happened but now, he says he wishes he hadn't because the footprint has become a shrine and my interest in it borders on obsession. Once, he lost his temper and threatened to stamp it into the ground. That would be the end of it, he said. That would be the end of us, I told him. He's said nothing more about it since, but I've taken a precautionary photograph on my mobile phone in case one day when I push back the beans the footprint is no longer there. I don't think George would ever destroy it but unless I keep vigil twenty-four hours a day, other things could happen. The birds could have a dust bath in the soil or, worse still, the neighbour's cat could use that patch of ground as a toilet. I think of myself as a gentle soul, but I swear I would kill the cat with my own hands if that happened. Although rain isn't forecast, I fetch the frame from the greenhouse and position it over the footprint. It makes me feel like I'm protecting her even though I know it's too late.

*

I spend hours thinking through the different stages of Emma's life. When she was a tiny baby I'd hover over her cot, anxious that she might stop breathing as she slept. Once she could walk, I worried about other hazards—double-decker buses, steps, bleach, objects which could be popped into small mouths. I took what I thought to be reasonable precautions against the dangers my child might encounter. Anything deemed to be harmful was put out of reach; stair-guards were fitted in the hall and on the landing; safety locks were fitted on cupboards; baby reins connected me to my young daughter whenever we walked beyond the house and garden. As a teenager there were new worries. As far as I know, she never experimented with recreational drugs, and I only ever saw her slightly tipsy after drinking alcohol. Then she became an adult and the responsibility for risk-assessing her life passed from me to her. She was healthy, successful at work and had a good social life. All appeared to be well. So much for appearances.

'Sorry for your loss,' people used to say after it happened. The expression riled me at the time. To have lost someone sounds careless, like it could have been avoided with a little more attention. Now, the sense of loss is buried deep within me. If I'd been more watchful over her, I'm certain she would still be here. I should have spotted that all was not well and probed more when she told me she was fine. I continue to have nightmares about the blurred black shapes of the two police officers who stood on the other side of the mottled glass of our front door, waiting for it to be opened. When they said Emma had been found in the river, I knew instinctively what she had done. As a child she developed a fascination for the bridge. George used to take her to the river where the two of them ate ice cream as they watched it being built. That's something I think about a lot.

*

At three o'clock I go back to the patio. George comes out of the back door with two steaming mugs. He's finished cleaning the paving slabs closest to the house and moved the table and chairs back into position. I remember when he laid the slabs. Emma was less than a year old, crawling around the carpet and watching him through the French windows.

'Looks better, eh?' he asks, nodding towards his work.

'It does,' I tell him, even though the difference is negligible.

'I've missed a few bits,' he says, looking at the ground and pointing with his index finger.

I notice his fingernail has been bitten so low there is very little left. The skin around the remnant of nail is ragged and raw. It looks out of place on his big, solid hand. My throat tightens and I feel an unexpected flicker of tenderness for him. When I reach across the space between us, he looks at me warily. I close my fingers over his and squeeze them gently. After a moment he squeezes mine back.

'You've done a good job, love,' I say, curling my hand into his.

He draws in a deep breath. We sit in silence, hand in hand, watching the sparrows as they bob around the garden with nesting materials in their beaks.

I Wanted to be a Bluesman
David Joseph

Every time I woke up after a storm, I thought of my brother. We grew up here, in this little fishing village, where the days are long, and people's lives are small. This was the place we were raised, the life we were born into. Dad worked the fishing boats with the men, and Mom taught at the tiny schoolhouse here.

We never left the village, not for anything. There were no trips to the city. No exotic vacations or even dull ones. We shopped at the local market and spent our days and nights in the village. Depending on how you looked at it, we either lived in a detached paradise or an isolated prison. Maybe both. But our contact with the outside world was limited. Dad said we weren't missing anything.

Our one link to the world beyond our small village was the radio, the strange box with frequencies that sat between our beds, with words and music leaking out of it each night as we went to sleep. Looking back today, with all of our fingertip technology, it's impossible to fathom just how important it was to have a radio. Without it, we'd never have heard the news or even known what the voice of the President of The United States sounded like. But what the radio brought us more than anything else was music.

This music we listened to on the radio was different from the music we'd heard in school, the classical music we'd heard in school. There was nothing wrong with classical music, of course, but it didn't speak to us, at least not most of us. And when our teacher placed that needle on a vinyl record in class, we often found ourselves dozing off, lulled to sleep by the syncopated rhythm of the crackling needle, as the record spun.

Listening to music on the radio was just the opposite. It was an awakening, a sonic stimulant, a desperate plea even, and we felt our bodies come to life the moment we heard it. That sound. It was something different. Something new. Something that reflected us, where we were, who we were, how we lived—all without confining us to it. This music was determined and passionate, and it was often played by black musicians. Today, we'd be told to call them African American, but when we were growing up, they were black, and we were white.

Sure, there was Sinatra and Bing Cosby and Mel Torme and plenty of white artists. But when we heard Howlin' Wolf or Muddy Waters or Jimmy Reed steamroll over the airwaves, the windows in our bedroom shook, and so did we. This music had teeth. It had guts. It dripped with sweat, and it bled, just like us.

Our parents didn't like the music, this music from the Mississippi Delta or Chicago or other parts of America that were foreign to them, and they didn't particularly like us listening to it. I'm not really sure why, but I'm not going to blame them. Not here and not now. I'm just going to say that they didn't understand it, and nothing we said could explain it to them. Nothing at all, no matter how hard we tried. My brother told me that they'd never get it. At the time, I didn't believe him, but he was right.

Sometimes, as we listened to those throaty voices and heard those squealing guitars, we'd lay in the dark, in our beds, and smile. I couldn't see my brother's face in the dark, but I didn't have to see it to know he was smiling. There was just something so satisfying in the music. And even if the songs were about hardship, pain, and the difficulties life might bring, they filled us with hope, left us with a feeling of possibility, which was something that wasn't easy to come by in our village. You could only get there if you dreamed, really dreamed, and these songs on the radio allowed us to do just that.

Since I knew mom and dad weren't fans of the music we listened to, I would try and keep the volume down to a reasonable level out of respect for them. But my brother would reach over from his bed and twist the dial in the opposite direction. He said the music was meant to be played loud, and that it was our duty to play it loud out of respect for the music. Eventually, mom would yell for us to turn it down and we would, but not until after my brother had attempted to blow the roof off the place, if only for a moment.

I bought my first guitar when I was sixteen. I'd finally scrounged up enough money from cleaning the fishing boats to buy one. It was an acoustic guitar, made from swamp ash wood, and I was determined to learn how to play the blues. My father couldn't believe I had chosen to spend my money on a guitar or, rather, 'wasted' my money on it as he put it. Mom said I was free to spend it however I wanted, and my brother just laughed.

'You'll never be able to play that thing,' he said. 'Not like those guys. And besides, you're not black.'

'We'll see,' I said.

Although I wanted to tell him he was wrong about me learning to play, I knew I'd have to prove it. That was the only way, and there was no sense arguing with him. There was never any sense arguing with him, about anything, when he had his mind made up. And he had his mind made up about this. As far as he was concerned, I was a fool.

To be perfectly honest, I wasn't at all sure I could learn to play the guitar either. After all, there were no musicians in our family, and I'd never displayed any type of music ability. Of course, I wasn't black either and, if that was a prerequisite for being able to play the blues, well, then I was doomed.

For the time being, though, I just decided to keep quiet. What was the use in fighting? It seemed rather pointless, and I would just have to be patient. Nobody in our house believed in me or was going to support me in this pursuit. So, I checked a book out of the library on how to play the guitar, and I got to work, learning where to place my fingers on the strings. That's how I did it, and I taught myself. I made sure to learn how to play chords and fingerpick too. Of course, I made tons of mistakes. But one thing I never did was play the guitar when my brother was around. Not ever. He would surely have been merciless, and I wasn't willing to give him the satisfaction.

Somehow, though, I had already learned those songs, those songs we listened to, and they were now embedded in my soul, way down deep, deeper than I even knew. I could remember them word for word, and I could spot the ache in Muddy Water's voice or pick out the wail in B.B King's guitar. All these sounds had been catalogued in my memory, and I heard them inside my head. I also learned that I had a better ear than

I might have thought, and my rhythm wasn't bad either. I just kept playing, practicing, relentlessly, without mentioning it to anyone.

This was around the time my brother was preparing to graduate from high school. Mom and dad wanted him to go to college if he wasn't going to work on the fishing boats, but he had other ideas. He told us that a friend of his, who was one year older than him, had made it to California.

'He says they're giving away jobs there,' my brother told my parents, who clearly disapproved.

It was one thing to dream of making it to Boston or Chicago, as improbable as that was. But California, that was truly beyond the realm of comprehension, not to mention it being well beyond the moral and spiritual realm my parents had existed in for their entire lives.

'How you planning to get to California?' my father snapped one day.

'Bus ticket. Using the money I saved from working on the fishing boats,' he said. 'Since I didn't waste it on a worthless guitar.'

My father looked at me disapprovingly, and I couldn't be sure which one of his sons had disappointed him more. He clearly disapproved of California and everything it stood for, but he was in agreement with my brother's assertion that I had not spent my money wisely.

*

The night before my brother left for California, there was a terrible storm outside. We lay in our room, while the thunder crashed, without saying a word. My brother even let me choose the radio station, and he didn't try and turn it up either. He just sat there in his bed, with his hands behind his head, breathing, pulling the air deep into his lungs and letting it out, while the storm raged outside, and the music played on.

I couldn't pretend that my brother wasn't different, different from me that is. He surely was, and we rarely saw eye to eye. But he was my big brother, and I still idolized him. We'd shared that bedroom in our small house in this little fishing village all our lives. And we'd fallen asleep listening to the radio together every night for as long as I could remember.

'Wanted you to know that you can keep the radio,' he said. 'I mean, when I go. It's yours.'

'Thanks,' I said.

'Sure,' he said. 'Least I can do, seeing as I'm leaving you here in this boring town.'

'Is that why you're leaving?' I asked. 'Because you're bored?'

'That and a hundred other reasons,' he said. 'Haven't you been listening to the songs?'

'What do you mean?' I asked.

'I've got to get out of here,' he insisted. 'I've got to break free, of this place, this life, of Mom and Dad, all of it. I can't be trapped here, not forever, not anymore. It's like Howlin' Wolf said, *'I'm gonna get up in the morning / Hit the Highway 49.'* That what I've got to do. Hit the highway and head west. I just know it. I can feel it.'

We sat quietly a bit longer. I wasn't sure what to say, but I'd never heard my brother talk with so much passion. Oh, we'd listened to the songs together, but I hadn't realized that he'd been building up energy, building up courage, real courage, that the songs had taken him places, places he had to go and could never come back from. Not ever.

'Well, at least you still have your guitar,' he said, after a long silence. 'Maybe now you'll learn how to play it.'

'I know how to play it,' I said plainly.

'What are you talking about?' he said. 'I've never seen you pick that thing up. Not even once. All it's done is collect dust in that closet.'

I slid my feet over the side of my bed and sat up facing my brother without saying a word. I'm not sure why I did it or chose to do it or did it at that moment. Perhaps it was because his remarks had annoyed me, even though he hadn't meant to, not really, anyway. Or maybe it was because he was leaving the next morning and I wondered if this might be my last chance. Whatever the reason, I was going to do it.

So, I stood up in the dark and walked across the thick carpet toward the closet. It was pitch black in the room, but the lights had been out long enough for my eyes to adjust. Besides, I could make my way around our tiny space with my eyes closed, so long as my brother hadn't left anything on the floor.

When I got to the closet, I reached for the doorknob, pulled the heavy, wooden door open, and bent down in order to reach into the back corner under our hanging clothes. That was where I kept my guitar, and

I grabbed it by the neck and walked back over to my bed. I sat down on the edge, with it fastened to my hands like a real bluesman.

'What do you think happens now?' laughed my brother. 'You think that thing just plays itself?'

I heard him, but not really. I wasn't listening. Not to him. Not anymore. I just sat there, tuning my guitar in the dark. I didn't need a tuner, not as long as I could hear the strings, and I twisted the ends and plucked them until it was perfectly in tune. The radio was still playing, and I waited for the next song to come on, while I got comfortable. I noticed my brother had now sat up and was facing me, but we didn't exchange words.

Just then, the Howlin' Wolf's song, *Goin Home,* was spun over the airwaves. By now I had gotten good, very good, and I could play along, at least marginally, with any song on the radio by ear. I closed my eyes, took a deep breath and began to play, picking off notes in the dark while the music poured out of the radio and Howlin' Wolf sung:

Going back home, going back home
Got to go home, got to go home
Got to go home, got to go home
Where I, where I was born

I just kept playing, with my eyes closed and my head crooked over the guitar, and I noticed my brother had even turned up the radio and was now slapping his knee. I just concentrated on the notes and kept playing until the song ended and the DJ's voice came on over the radio. Afterwards I noticed I was out of breath, from the tension I suppose, even though I hadn't sung a word. I set the guitar against the side of my bed and put my head in my hands until I felt my brother reach across on grab my left shoulder with his right hand.

'Well, goddamn,' he said. 'We got ourselves a bluesman. Blues guitar anyway. We got ourselves a *real* bluesman, a damn white bluesman, but a bluesman nonetheless.'

He went on like this for few minutes, while I smiled in the dark. He couldn't see my face, but I think he knew I was smiling.

'Thanks,' I said, before getting up and returning the guitar to the back of our closet.

I walked to the bed and lay on my back again, this time staring at the ceiling. A Jimmy Reed song was playing on the radio now, and I reached over to turn the volume dial back down to a normal level. We both just lay there in our beds, without saying a word for the rest of the night, until we fell asleep alongside one another.

All these years we'd been listening to the radio together each night before bed, discovering this great music, this music from another place, that we weren't going to hear in our town. We felt like explorers, real explorers, who'd discovered something, not so much a new territory, but a secret. A great secret. The music unlocked parts of our being we didn't even know were there.

The songs were powerful. They got inside us, spoke to us, challenged us. They were world weary and modern all at once, and we were left, each of us, to determine what we were going to do, how we were going to live, to be, now that we had heard those songs.

And yet, while we listened to the same songs, we heard them differently. We brought different parts of ourselves, and parts of ourselves that were different. And where my brother could never stop thinking about Howlin' Wolf telling him to *hit the highway,* all I heard was a man who just wanted to 'go home'.

When I woke up the next morning, the storm had passed. My brother was gone. All these years later, I'm still here.

A Song from a Different Room
Gwen Williams

The pink wafers are on a plate on the table. A meeting is going to start in my dining room. A kind of talking meal not an eating one. Linda opens the door and in walks a man covered in thin stripes. A woman I have not seen before or her red coat. Linda, the stripey man and the woman scrape back chairs and sit round our table looking at the pink wafers my best tasting ones when they gently crack in my gums. I have no teeth.

I watch from the doorway – a safe spot between this room and that room. They turn and look at me. I look away. Hello, Lizzie, they say and stare and curl their mouths. Their eyes travel past me and say 'problem.' Their voices are a noise inside my head a buzzing like the dangerous cars rushing past our place. Then comes a sound like when I drop a cup crash on the floor or a knife crack on the kitchen floor.

Cutz says the striped man.

Naming Cutz makes them shake their heads. Does the word hurt them as it hurts me? Makes me pull my sleeve, makes me nod my head and let my tongue stick out. Scratch myself to make sure I am still here. Listening, not listening, not getting through. Fluffy melting words are gentle. Breeze, blossoms, feather, custard, I love custard, wafer is good. Biscuit too sharp.

I can't have a pink wafer. I'm on a diet.

Care-plan says so.

So, the talking meal today is about Cutz. Who is this Cutz? I can tell she or he is bad and no good will come of it. It will mean less of something for me. Their eyes hot as a tea mug then cold as wet spuds tell me so. 'Leo's too cossly.' I hear new woman in red jacket say and I guess they mean going to Leo's place for music will have to stop.

Linda who guards me has turned her face into a cat shape and is whispering low. I don't understand many words, but I know that Linda the Guardian who takes me to Leo's room has made a disliking face and I already know she doesn't like going there. She's cross in the blue wheeled car. Loud thundering comes from the front making Linda nod her head fast and my ears sting.

Once Linda went too fast and a fierce type of man in black and white and shining buttons waved and made her stop and leaned through the window shouting, 'Yore speed, madam.' Linda says 'Swayss o time' to go to Leo's and cruel to me because I, what is it? get upset there. She knows this because I thump my side and squeal. Leo mimics me she says, it's disrespectful, abuse even. No Linda, I am not squealing that is me singing and beating rhythm.

I turn my back on all of them and noisy pointless meal of words meaning now one thing then another different thing. Far too many when one sound or one hand sign would do. Nothing new is ever said. I hobble to my safe spot, the still bit by the main door where no-one one stays only come in and go out. I think how Leo looks like Dad. When I think about him it's like a ghost might tell someone a message, in smells, in sounds, in faces, in…sighs.

I'm like a bee dancing to other bees or the scent that passes from spider to spider to drive them crazy in the dark. I chew my empty lips and do quick nods. This helps. You only have to watch me to know I am a muddled one. The shiny glass on the wall holds that well known face again with hollows under the dark eyes and topped with silvery strands. This is the familiar which used to be in the blue dress with a swinging mop of brown on top. It came here with me from the Hospital of Echoes to this small hut. Its followed me all the way. What makes it change so? First grew bigger and bigger. Now growing smaller and paler every light time.

*

Dad's words didn't hurt. I still keep in my head his leather face, blurry a bit now. Softness of his voice and gentleness of face. I tried to talk once upon a time, but I was like an afraid creature going ootzi-wootzi-fzty-hoytzee like that brown bird outside who tells the day to start…. when I have not knocked off to not-there-ness through all the lovely dark quiet time. My time in the box alone resting from the people in the place.

When I used to see Dad, I would run at him grinning and so would he be curving up his mouth and say, 'hello Lizzie' and make a hearty ha ha at me.

Then I would grab his big hand rough with soil and doing things and pull him along to walk with me, just get away from others our feet the same, this one that one. He would go 'steady-on-lass.'

Long ago, there was someone called Mum when I was in the great Hospital of Echoes, but her smile was sad and faraway and flat like that white pudding we had yesterday. I knew that her heart was not ticking for me, and she wanted to go away. She was there from a having to be there like me and Care-plan but didn't like it. Didn't like me.

I could nearly taste her smell that was sharp like apple and sweet as too much chocolate. I think it was a rare smell that people call 'cossly'. Her eyes were empty like an eaten soup. Her hands were the smooth hands of someone who had stopped doing anything useful.

But she went off. Where do they go? That was before I lived in this small bricky space in a long, long line of empty spaces all cemented in together with two others in wheelchairs who ran over my foot. Mum never found her way here. She was gone before I left Echo Hospital. Then Dad was all to myself. There was no one but us. If there were others who belonged to us, they shunned us properly. They probably thought no point in visiting someone who would not speak to them in words. Only look at them like a three-toed sloth. Their language after all is words. Unlike me whose first language is what I do. You only have to watch me to see that I am all movements like a dog's tail.

My Dad had the sounds of a gurgle of water and the warm smell of weary clothes and tobacco and sweets, of healthy earth and also, I didn't understand, a burny, smoked smell sometimes, dangerous to me and exciting.

People said country gentleman who went shooting. Sometimes large colourful birds with long tails would appear in the kitchen and lie still on the draining board. Then a stringy meal.

But not now because from his cottage with the garden in rows of green and brown he went to a big house like a hospital, with others, white and grey like him. He was tired. Sleepy tired like the familiar in the shiny glass when lots of others are about. His face had lines of deep brown and sometimes a bruise. Sometimes he looked serious and didn't say my name, Lizzie. Called me Emily instead. Mum's other name? One time, very purple marks with some green, from falling his Guardians told my Guardians. They brushed crumbs from his scumbly jumper and wiped spit and pudding off his face. And then I went no more to that place of sharp smell of wet pad.

The next thing, we took some black trousers home from a big shop and a dark jacket. Six Guardians brought me to a room of chairs in careful lines. I liked their tidy rows like Dad's garden and all around were people in black too. Some came up and pretended to know me. They knew my name but did not say their name. I had never seen them before. 'Cousins'— my Guardians said and stood around me just in case. 'Uncles, Aunts.' They all had wipes to dry off their rainy faces. I have never rained on my face. Were they sad because they had no Guardians? They had to carry their own bag and drive their own risky cars. Sad men, serious men speaking on a strange stage and Dad had not arrived. So I ran to the door at the back and went looking for him arriving and my Guardians let me stay out because there was a windy box making wheezing sounds like strangled air that scared me. It was struggling not to break.

*

We had a doughnut thing of flowers with us but did not give it to anyone. The Guardians left it on the ground. They forgot to bring it home. I tried to show them. It was red and white and smelled of dead plants. They said come on Lizzie. Dad never came. Where was he?

They have still not found him. I went to the shadow of the darkest corner of the noisy telly room and curled up quietly. Dad did not come with his lovely smile for me. He left me. Like Mum. Did he go to live with her instead? No-one knows where he is.

I sat in the corner curled up for a long time. Light and dark took turns to gather round me. It helped. I got used to the stab…stab…stab in my belly. And then another Dad type turned up.

A knock at the door one day and in squealed a new wheelchair and I saw a younger sort of Dad. Handsome with hair like a brush. Dark color of hair and smelling chocolaty and slightly of a spicy stew. His face too thin for his long, long grin. He put out his hand to me and mine went halfway there but the fingers were not sure yet. 'Hello Lizzie, I'm Match-You' whatever that means. He spoke slowly as if it was a difficult thing he tried to do, and I liked that. And with a bit of a twist to his lop-sided slippery mouth which made me soften.

Soon after he rolled in, I came right out of my corner and into the middle of the room and sat with Match-you. He put out his hand again and I held his thumb very tight so hard that he went 'Ow' and I made a ha ha and did it again.

We began to learn each other's language. Better than the Guardians learned. I heard new sounds and kept them in my head like 'love' and 'pretty' and 'kind'. Words they were that Match-You said to me every day. 'We're a good team,' said Match-You and this meant doing things between us like sneak chocolate from the fridge where the Guardians 'stashed ' it. Match-You looked out and I would steal. He had a special big-wheeled car with a 'suitable seat' for me and we went on outings now which he called 'dates' and the Guardians called 'activities.' We went to big houses like Hospital and gardens and crunched on gravel. We always had a Guardian because I couldn't push wheelchair or find my way or give people the right small metal bits that get you tea and sweets and your favourite cake.

When we tried to go into big houses I would stop and turn around and not move. I have kept in my mind cross people from when the shiny wall thing held a familiar who had teeth then and a blue bag of a dress on and swinging brown hair. I was bad then. I bit a Guardian. He came too close, much too close, tickling me in my pants. and to stop me biting again I fell asleep and woke and only had gums. No more going in big houses for me Guardians. And Match-You's wheels would not go up the steps. On purpose, I think. Match-You said 'Soakay'

We liked to go home and sit on the sofa side by side pulled together by that sort of smell like cats do and touch hands and faces while the Guardians were looking away or chatting about their own men in cross voices eyebrows down or changing over shifts as they called it.

I was never cross with my man Match-You. He was not shit like the Guardians' men-types. My days were waiting at the window when he went to work at day centre Greenwood and full of his grin and huge Ha Ha when he came home. Even the noisy screen in the telly room was not so painful when he was there and the big-faced man saying 'Look-at-me-you-scum-grow-a-pair.'

But the cold times came around. Match-You started watering from his red nose and making a hoovering sound deep down inside his shirt. He went white then very purple. He stayed in bed and a black bag man came. This is always a bad sign. He put Match-You into a white van with yellow squares. The word Hospital so I knew no good would come of this. I went back into the corner and curled up waiting for him to come home.

And waited and waited. But I had to put on black trousers again and the jacket and the Guardians forgot another doughnut of flowers on the ground.

Empty days in my corner curled up still and silent. The angry man shouting at dirty types on the screen every morning. I turned my back on him. The Guardians left me there with nothing to do and no-one. Dad and Match-You didn't like me. Perhaps were with each other?

Until man number Three, Leo or a sound like Hello. Leo, Hello. He has a special noise museum. There are special sounds there and special cutlery to have a music meal. Some he hits the air with and makes a thud…thud…thud. Some he shakes tin…tin…tinny jangling, others he plucks with a special shaped comb, and it goes 'dowowowowow'. My best is a long stripey table with teeth of black and white. It brings gentle pearly ripples and sparkling waterfalls and draws me in against my will. I jingle tingle inside and little waves dance to the shore. Makes me want to know all about it. But turn away at first. Not getting close to man number Three and end up with flowery ring forgotten on the ground and invisible ache in the corner.

They don't want to, but Care-plan says the Guardians must bring me here time after time after time and Leo-Hello sounds what he calls music. Care-plan says what I have to do with my life. Somehow Leo knows that I like the waterfall table. He speaks gently. It doesn't hurt me and often he uses up and down language called, *Song,* which I get.

He makes a sound like Hollowlizzie going up three stairs. Yesterday I forgot myself and turned towards him. Leo-Hello held out his hand. When I dared to touch his hand, it was tough and rough like Dad's hand and my fingers followed it pulling out from my belly the brave earth belly of me and I sat down on the long seat next to Leo- Hello for ten whole moments. He touched the teeth and from nowhere ripples sounded. He stopped. He looked at me. I took his rough hand and put it back on the teeth. I have not done this before. He musicked again and was grinning. Linda didn't see. She didn't know head down tap tapping at a small metal instrument. Making her music?

*

This language is strange like the word the cat makes and cars howl softly and breeze whining. I forget myself and let out wild hums and Leo-Hello plays it on the white teeth and sings the three stairs to Hello Lizzie. I try him out on another hum higher and he follows me, and I rat a tat on my leg and soon we are playing a game, and he is in my language nearly. A good team. And Linda says too soon 'Time to go. Short staffed.'

And I am starting to see that it all must mean something. So many funny feelings tickle me, tease me, hit me and without having pains in my body I can feel drops of cold sorrow running down my face. Leo-Hello sees and with a hankie smelling of lemons he wipes my face with his arm round my shoulders which I hate but I let his hand stay. The Guardians say I am autistic. Sev-ear-lee. But I let him hug me imagine it's Dad or Match-You and for a tick for a moment it is a gleaming ray of light when I feel—someone can see me, someone can get me, human and living and myself. In the open space—with Leo-Hello who is ready to learn my language.

I tell the familiar in the mirror who has been with me all my life I have found another one of us.

The Guardians round the table are getting up. Nodding. That means no more Leo-Hello for me, I guess.

'Damn Cutz,' the striped man sings.

Ouch. The woman in the red coat has eaten all the pink wafers.

Starfish
Sheila Killian

Lookit, I'm not saying I can explain everything that happened. I just walked into Margie's Bar on a Friday afternoon trying to pretend I hadn't been away for ten years. Trying to look local in this ridiculous dress. So yeah, I was holding my breath a bit, what of it? It's not as easy as you'd think, coming home.

The place was nearly empty. I ordered a pint from the young one behind the bar and sat in the corner, window light falling on my table, glimmering the glass like an Instagram post. I don't even drink Guinness. You wouldn't, in London. It's not the done thing for women like me.

The place hadn't changed much. Davy must have put that big screen up when he took over from his Mam, but everything else looked the same: scuffed vinyl on the bench seats, faded green fabric on low wooden stools, a lopsided No Smoking sign with an Irish flag and a Mayo one askew behind the frame. The pint was good. I exhaled, took out my phone and started scrolling.

Someone had posted photos from the wedding already and I swiped through them all, careful not to hit like. She didn't need a filter, dreamy white silk up among the dune grass, her face perfect, eyes glittering like a doll's, unreadable. And he was there, of course, always just behind her, making himself her background. I made myself look at his face. He looked well with that dark brush of stubble, and he filled his dress shirt like an athlete. The skinny boy he used to be flashed into my mind, moonlight on his back running into the sea. I was cold, suddenly, as though that salty wind was still circling around me. I took another drink from my pint. Looked up.

And there she was. Impossible and young, leaning over the end of the bar to be served, wearing cropped jeans that looked familiar because they were, because that's all we wore that long summer—stripey t-shirts and cut-off denims, poor man's Vans from Penneys, thinking we were cool. I couldn't see her face. The barmaid handed her a can of Fanta and she walked straight out the back door. Something silver at her left wrist caught the light.

Straight away I was up and following. I nearly turned back for my phone, half thinking I could take a photograph. Anyway, I don't have anything like that. It's only a memory, but I'm fairly sure it happened.

I should start at the beginning, shouldn't I? Sarah was my first friend when we moved here to Inishawl. I was five. I used to go to her house after school, her Mam would pick both of us up, and sometimes I stayed for dinner if my Da wasn't home. Her house wasn't like mine. There was sponge cake and ice cream any time you wanted, not just Sundays. There were big bowls of fruit and books made for children and toys that didn't come from distant cousins and second-hand shops. She had new clothes all the time. There was a Da who came home at teatime with clean nails, and a mother who made bread and wore perfume and smiled. Any mother would have done for me. Mine died, and Da, well, he tried, you know? He thought moving here would help. But it wasn't in him to rear me.

Me and Sarah, though. We were for each other from the start. I remember a céili in the yard behind the school. There was a part where you had to cross hands, face your partner and spin, so we did, Sarah and me. We held tight, went around like a top, spinning and spinning until we were gasping and laughing and dizzy. I could hear people telling us to slow down, to be careful, but the world was going round so fast that all we could see was each other, her laughing face all mine. She was closer to me than anyone. She was the best thing.

We sat together, learned together. Sarah called me a starfish when we learned about them in biology. They just lay their eggs out into the sea, and the babies grow up wild.

'Like you.'

'You mean motherless?'

'I mean brilliant, Meg. They live in the sea all the time, and if they get hurt, they can grow a whole new arm.'

'I can't do that.'

'But you swim like them.'

That was true. I loved to swim, loved to be out of my depth, to let myself sink down, searching with my toes and to not feel the sand underneath me and then kick back and float, arms wide to the sky. Always alone because Sarah was a lousy swimmer. She wasn't afraid of the water. She just wasn't strong.

'And they're beautiful, Meg, like you.'

'And you.'

So, the first time we both had money, we went to Westport on the bus and bought starfish charms to put on our cheap bracelets. She wore hers every day. I never took mine off. It was a promise forged in silver plate.

We were such friends for so long, but it took us no time at all to become strangers.

At the start of Leaving Cert year, we decided to get matching tattoos as soon as we turned eighteen. We sketched them out. Well, she did. She was the artistic one. A little starfish with five stiff arms to replace our tarnished charms. I traced hers, and I stuck it on the wall of my bedroom. We'd doodle them on the margins of our books. I drew one on every one of my exam papers, for luck. Sarah said she did too, but of course you can't know, can you?

Then it was August, school was over, and we were on the edge of new things. Anything could happen. We were a double act for that summer, playing cool in Margie's backyard, cadging cigarettes that we could barely smoke and flirting with the summer boys. Bold as brass, my Dad would say. And just as shiny, I used to think. We went everywhere together, laughing too loud on the rusty fairground rides, being ironic about it, pretending we were only pretending to love it because we were plainly so cool, and way too grown up for that. We drank a little beer sometimes, though not much. Sarah was a lightweight. Some nights we'd just lie on the beach with the tide out and the moon rising, waves hissing and hushing, stars blinking above us.

Then he came along. There were lots of boys that summer, passing through, but he was the most beautiful. His hair was straggly in the way of surfers. He wore long shorts even in bad weather, and a knotted leather cord on his wrist. His sandy skin looked delicious. He drew attention without seeming to try, ragged in a way that seemed really careless, not like the hair-gel local lads who were always checking the mirror when they thought you weren't looking. When we saw him first, rolling a smoke with his tanned fingers, his broken nails, we decided to reel him in.

Yeah, we. It was both of us. Me and Sarah. I mean, she saw him first, but we set out together and went after him. I'm nearly sure that's what I believed then. She wouldn't see it like that, I suppose. All we did that first night was smoke his rollies and laugh at his jokes. But there came a point in the evening when we stopped working together, when we both knew that we both wanted him, and without saying a word, we were cutting across each other, competing for the first time in our lives. I suppose, looking back, he must have liked it. At the time I didn't care what he felt. I just knew I was in a race, and I had to win.

And I did. Sarah went off with her aunt to Roundstone for a week, and while she was gone, him and me became a thing. I mean nothing really happened. There were a few sweet nights of swimming together way out in the deep water, then back to the beach, burning the cardboard the beer came in and calling it a campfire. Leaning back into his warmth on the damp sand. Drinking a little vodka for the first time. I say nothing happened, but I felt safe and loved in the boldness of the beach at night.

One night he found one, a real starfish, and he held it out to me. It was small and curling on the palm of his hand.

'For me?'

'You can't keep them.'

'Why not?'

'They die.'

He laughed, and I remember his arm arching back as he threw it into the sea. I ran into the waves, but it was gone.

Then Sarah came back, and we joined the summer kids again, hanging out behind Margie's most evenings and crossing over to the strand after closing time. I wasn't his anymore.

But then it was him and Sarah, she laughing up at him, me on the edge of the crowd. All my own laughter dried up. It wasn't so much him. I mean I fancied him, but not like before. I didn't want anyone who didn't want me. It was her I missed. With her I could go anywhere.

Without her, when he took her attention away, I was just me, nothing special. There was suddenly nothing to do.

I need to be clear. I knew she didn't try to steal him from me, but that didn't help. So, I watched them, searching for a crack, for a way to break it up and get things back to normal. Look, I know how it sounds. I know now, but I was seventeen, all right? It didn't feel like a bad thing.

The night before the Leaving Cert results, I saw him reach for Sarah's left wrist.

'What's this?'

He held up her starfish charm. I pulled down my sleeve a bit to hide mine. Hadn't he seen it?

'My lucky charm,' she said, and she smiled right at me, all light.

He turned it over.

'It's falling apart, isn't it? Maybe you could get it fixed up if it matters to you?'

'We don't need to. We're getting a tattoo.'

I was stupid, blurting it out like that, a kid looking for attention. Sarah's eyes widened just for a second. He dropped her wrist, and ignored me, all eyes still on Sarah.

'You don't strike me as the tattoo type.'

'I'm not. That's just a thing we used to say, you know, in school.'

She laughed. I got up and looked away. I went straight in to the bar and bought two naggins. Davy knew I was underage, but he always looked after me. In the bathroom, I poured some in my can of Fanta.

Then we were on the beach, five of us. The lads went running into the sea. It was me and Sarah again under the dunes.

'Hey, I'm sorry, Meg.'

'For what?'

'For, you know. The tattoo and everything. You know my folks would never let me—'

'Oh, you're grand.' I gulped my drink. The vodka was kicking in. She was watching the lads, far out now, shouting to each other in bravado. The waves were high, and the tide was turning. I took the first naggin from my pocket and emptied it into my can. I held the second one out to her.

'Want some?'

It wasn't a peace offering. I did, for a long time, pretend it was. But I knew she couldn't hold her drink, and quickly, before she could say yes or no, before the others came back, I reached for her can and spiked it, smiling, swirling it round to mix it up so she wouldn't taste all the vodka at first, so she wouldn't know how much I'd put in. I never wanted her to come to any harm. I don't know what I wanted, maybe to make her less perfect? Maybe to rat her out to her Mam? I didn't have a plan, but it wasn't kindness, I know that. And it wasn't jealousy either. More like rage.

'Starfish are stupid anyway,' pulling the charm from my wrist and turning it over in my hand. She lifted her can and drank.

'No, they're amazing,' she said, leaning back on her elbows. 'That thing with growing a broken arm back. Incredible.'

'Sometimes they break off their own arms, you know.'

'On purpose?'

I nodded.

'Only if they have to. If they're hurt and need to get free again.'

She said nothing. She was drinking again, too fast for the amount of vodka I put in, but she liked it.

'And they're beautiful,' I said.

But she didn't answer 'like you' the way she used to. She didn't answer at all. She sat up straight and looked over the waves where the three lads were far out, surely out of their depth.

'You have to throw them back, you know. If you find one.'

I looked at her sharply. Did she hear that from him?

'Come on, then,' I said, without thinking too hard. 'Let's do it.'

I helped her up and she wobbled down to the water's edge, and I showed her my charm in my open hand and then arched my arm back and flung it as far as I could, into the surf.

I watched her wade in, and I didn't follow. I turned back so she wouldn't see my face.

He saved her, of course. I was a mess by then, crying like a child. The moon had come out, gleaming on the sea and I remember Sarah, floppy on the sand and then breathing. Alive.

He was sure I tried to kill her, but it wasn't my fault she nearly died. Not all my fault. I stayed out all night, woke alone on the dunes, feeling like dirt. I'd have given anything to say I was sorry, but nobody was talking to me by then, and he was always there so I couldn't get near Sarah.

That was the end it. I went to college and then London, where I made new shiny friends who laugh at my jokes, laugh sometimes even when I don't think I'm being funny. They don't really know what part of Ireland I'm from. There's no trace of my old accent anyway. It's new, like everything else about me. I'm paid way too much for what I do. My apartment is tasteful and expensive. I date a bit but nothing sticks. I run twice a week in Hyde Park. I hate running. I never swim. I have become a woman in a magazine.

Except it's boring, isn't it? Everyone is more or less the same in my world. Nobody laughs until they hiccup. Nobody looks me right in the eye like she used to.

One night I saw a Netflix documentary about starfish. They call them sea stars now. I like that name better.

It took me years to stalk Sarah out on the socials. She wasn't hard to find, still living in Inishawl, teaching in that tiny school. That's how I found out she got engaged. How I found out it was to him. How I came to see his face again, older, fuller, his eyes more blue than before. How I found out about his job that took him to London sometimes.

It was easy. I could see where he stayed when he was there. So I took to going there too, drinking in the lobby, lying in wait, ready to fake surprise when we bumped into each other at the door. I thought I could charm him back. In real life, when he finally showed up, he was lumpier than his photos, and there was a looseness about his walk that marked him off as not belonging. I watched him dragging his cheap overnight case to reception to check in, and I slipped out the door behind him.

After that, I stopped stalking, but then came her friend request, no chat, just asking for my address, and the wedding invitation arrived the following week. 'Do come,' she wrote in the corner, with a starfish in place of the 'o.' The card was thick and soft so I could feel the indentation of her pen when I ran my fingers over the words.

I couldn't refuse, but it turns out I couldn't show up either. I bottled it, leaving late from Knock in my rented car so I missed the service, and then at the edge of town, where I could see cars gathering at the new hotel, I just kept driving straight out here to the quiet of Inishawl. And that's how I came to be dressed to the nines, following a ghost out the back door of Margie's to that yard where Sarah and me had spent those summer evenings, drumming our heels back against the whitewashed wall with sheer life, silver charms on our wrists, waiting for life to begin.

There was nobody there. She was gone, my ghost, whoever she was. But then I looked down and saw it beside a pot of struggling cornflowers, four arms curling clockwise and a gap where the fifth used to be. She was gone, my ghost, but the starfish, the sea star, that was real enough.

The barmaid said a gull must have dropped it, but I know a gift when I get one. I carried it like treasure across to the strand, the salty wind making my eyes water. It was a heaving sea, big slow waves and an undertow, and there was nobody out there. Nobody at all. Slowly, at the edge of the water, I lowered my hand under the surface and opened it. And then I let go.

Sunday Morning
Dell Keniper

When Sara was a child, Sundays were the coal dust days. When once a week the steel mill released a cloud of debris that no sun, no man-made light, could penetrate. One hour after first shift began the warning whistle blew, and when its shriek tore through the town everyone—the men, the women, the children, even the drunks—knew they had to find shelter and for the next several hours wherever they were was where they would be. The dust poured undaunted from the mill, spreading until the sky was gray. Too heavy to mingle with the clouds, the coal's chaff hovered fifteen feet above the ground, while a fine layer of soot floated lower, painting the faces of anyone who dared to go outside and dirtying the laundry that, too late remembered, was abandoned on the line. Years after the steel shuttered and the dust stopped, Sara still easily recalled the dismal sky, but more than the dark, she remembered the silence. How once a week the town didn't move. How it barely breathed. She thought of it now as she walked along Levin's Sunday morning streets, her arms hanging at her sides in defiance of the wind and the bloated clouds.

Down river, the air had been cleaner. As a child, Sara was taught that this made the people from those nicer towns weak. In Levin, they could handle a little dust. Just breathe it in and spit it out. In Levin, they endured. It was that simple. Black and white. Good and bad. But today, at twenty-three, Sara finally understood that things were never that clear. Good never stayed the good you learned as a kid, and bad became an amorphous thing—shifting and viscous. A monster in the closet. An occasional friend. She'd realized that sometimes allowances needed to be made and judgment withheld. Today was an example. It was a day of permission. A day of circumstances so big they changed it all.

Sara hadn't been home in five years, and in that time her childhood house had become a haven for red envelope past dues and stacks of bills. In the past, her mother had been a woman who suffered losses like a tree sheds its leaves—her jobs, two husbands—each a different type of autumn followed by some kind of spring. But at some point in the years Sara had been gone, in all the weeks she'd forgotten to call, something had changed. There had been a drought, an early freeze. And now that she'd finally returned, randomly, selfishly seeking nourishment of her own, she saw she shouldn't have relied on her mother's seasonality. The new growth she'd taken for granted had never come. Sara should have known better. She'd been raised to help without being asked; she knew the needs expressed in silence were the most important kind.

Sara passed the two-church intersection on Madison and Washington just as the choirs were warming up. The congregations, Catholic and Episcopalian, pretended to be different, but today Sara heard the same hymns and sleep-tight devotion ringing from both. She wondered what would happen if she ran into the houses of worship with worry in her eyes and voice. *Please.* In the pews, she imagined the faces of the people she used to know. Strangers now. More people she hadn't called. *Please.* She could tell them she'd been wrong to leave, wrong to act better than, wrong to pretend her failures weren't real just because they happened far away. *Please, please.* She was back now, she could tell them. There was so much money needed in so little time, and she didn't want to do what she was going to do. She could be different. She could ask for help before it was too late. Today was too late. Today she would have to do something. *Please.*

It was one, two, three blocks until she crossed the main straightaway in town and reached Riggers, Levin's only bar. She could see it already: a cement bunker with faded blue walls capped by a flat tarpaper roof and surrounded by a gravel lot whose uneven mounds of dirt and rock seemed to undulate with each of Sara's steps, right, left, up, down, ebb, flow. Eddie was in there. That's what Sara's mother said when she wasn't talking about money. When she wasn't asking Sara for help. When she said nothing, she mentioned Eddie. A man few would admit they knew and a provider of the necessities no one wanted to discuss.

Rigger's still maintained the twenty-four-hour schedule that started when the mill was full swing, which meant the bar was just as open at seven in the morning as it was at five at night, and the staff showed no more loyalty to a patron who ended their night with a drink than they did to one who started their day with the same. Eight a.m.? Two? It didn't matter. Beyond the blacked-out glass door and the neon beer signs, the hours were seconds disappearing in swallows, and the days and nights were exactly the same.

Inside, the air was stagnant, its moist atmosphere seasoned by the ripe scent of beer drippings and rotting limes. The room where Sara stood was lit by white Christmas lights wrapped around the liquor behind the bar while three low-hanging lamps dimly glowed over the booths in the back. Strands of silver tinsel dangled from the ceiling and weakly flickered, while in the middle of the bar's bare floor, two men stagger-danced to their own discordant rendition of *Jingle Bells*. Both noticed and then quickly disregarded Sara as she crossed toward the quieter, though still occupied, bar.

'I still say tear it down slow. In pieces. If that makes me puss, least I'll be safe,' said the blond man hunched at the bar, his back so low that his shirt seemed attached to the wood. Even without seeing his face, Sara could tell there was something misshapen about him. A bent nose to match his uneven shoulders or a scar that deformed without promising grit. The bartender, a towering redhead, grinned.

'Shitall, Steve. You even seen a pussy since Gail left?'

'Screw off, Ang.'

'I'm saying, think you'd recognize one?'

'Hell,' Steve said.

Besides the two dancing men, Steve (according to Ang), and Ang (according to Steve), there was only one other person there. If Sara's mother was right, it had to be Eddie. His pants were the same work-dirty shade of brown as those on the other men. His sweatshirt had the same scattered mix of patches and holes. But even with those interchangeable aspects, he looked different than the men around him. Instead of carrying defeat like Steve, who occupied the stool next to him, or the clownishness of the men caroling behind, Eddie seemed to own everything in the room. The wood beneath him and the bottles in front, the cement floor and the drop ceiling, the liquors, the beers, Angie,

Steve, and the singing boys. It was like the entire bar was his, as though it always had been and always would be.

'Get out,' Angie said clearly to Sara though her gaze remained on the glass she half-heartedly polished.

'I need Eddie,' Sara said, and then nothing else. The name hung in the air in front of her, heavy and solitary, pulling on her lips and dragging her closer to the bar.

Eddie turned and looked at Sara. 'You need me, huh?' he said, glancing at Steve. Steve looked at Angie, then shifted a stool over.

Angie slammed the glass on the bar, her irritation echoing throughout the room. Steve laughed. The problem was his bent nose, but also his sagging mouth and the slope of one eye.

'Get out,' Angie said again, this time staring at Sara. Her eyes were sharp.

'Maybe we should talk later,' Sara said. 'Or somewhere else.'

'Because of Ang? Nah. She's all bark. Aren't you, Ang?'

'You're pushing.'

'You don't like it anymore? Catch that, Steve? Ang's lost her taste.'

Eddie pointed at the two carolers in the corner, their voices, arms, and necks now stretched in an earnest *Hark, Hear the Bells*. 'Come on. You let those mutts stay.'

'I'll go.' Sara stood.

Eddie grabbed her hand. 'Not without one drink. You want her to stay, don't you, Steve?' Eddie smiled. His face was severe—all angle and bone—and his eyes were the murky color of honey, but it was his teeth that trapped Sara's attention. They were unlike any she'd seen before. His incisors were tiny, making his canines look sharper like he'd spent time grinding them against bark or bone. His left front tooth was turned and more translucent than the rest. Its edge was jagged from a broken corner that told the story of two fights—the first in which he'd lost the original and the second that broke its replacement. For the moment that Sara couldn't help but stare, she saw movement behind this gap, as though Eddie's tongue twitched slightly, quickly, continuously. She dropped her eyes. She didn't want to be sure.

'You gonna tell me your name?'

'Sara,' she said.

'Sara . . . Sara, Sara.' Eddie rolled the word around his mouth until it began to sound unlike a name and more like a barbaric act from a long-past time and place. *He sara'ed her straight to the bone.* 'Seems dumpy, you ask me. I'm going with Sweet Pea. Swear not to use it on anyone else.'

Steve sucked mucus from his nose to his throat, then swallowed it along with the last ice from his drink. 'Ang—' He shook his empty glass.

Angie broke her eyes from Eddie and grabbed a bottle of spiced rum from the shelf by her thighs. 'This one? Or you ready for the big-boy stuff?'

Steve pushed his glass forward. 'Careful, or I'll show you a big boy.' He pumped his hips. Angie smirked and poured. Eddie turned toward Sara. 'What do you want, Sweet Pea? Vodka cran? Rum and Diet Coke?'

'It's too early,' Sara said.

'Princess,' Steve muttered.

Sara looked at the men, the woman, and the darkness around her. She thought of why she was there in the first place. She remembered what she had to do. 'I'll take a regular Coke,' she said. 'And a vodka.'

Eddie slapped the bar. 'There it is, Ang. Two drinks for the lady and a vodka ice for me.'

Angie shook her head as she reached into the well, directing her disapproval at the glass she chose, the bottle she lifted, and the liquor that poured between the two. Once the drink was down, Angie paused, her breath held as though she was about to say something, but after a moment, she exhaled and filled a second glass with Coke. She placed it on the bar next to Sara's vodka. 'Watch these,' she said as she began Eddie's drink.

'Okay,' Sara said to no response.

After the drinks were down, a moment of reverence settled in the bar. Even the carolers seemed to respect it, shifting seamlessly into *Silent Night* and lowering their voices until the song became more lullaby than hymn. All could be calm, Sara thought, all bright. What she was going to do didn't have to change her. It wasn't forever. It could just be a choice she made. It could be forgotten, eventually. It wasn't for her. It was for her mother. Her family. It was important. It was only skin on skin.

'Don't be nervous,' Eddie said.

Sara nodded. 'My mother,' she started.

'Does she look like you?' Eddie smiled.

'She needs money.'

'There it is,' Steve said. 'Tell her how it works, Magic Man.'

The caroling had stopped, and the two singing men stood locked in an embrace. It was unclear if anger or love held them arm over arm and hands around the backs of necks.

'It's just economics,' Eddie said. 'Supply and demand.'

'Oldest sale in the books,' Steve said.

Eddie looked at Sara again. 'You'll be fine.'

'You'll get what you need,' Steve sang, evoking a glare from the taller of the two carolers behind him. An orange man—hair, hat, shirt.

'She's too young,' Angie muttered.

'Weren't you the same age, Ang? Didn't Ed help you?'

'He never helped me like that.'

'You sure?' Steve bounced his pelvis again.

'It's quieter in the back,' Eddie said to Sara. 'For the details.'

Sara looked over Steve's shoulder at the booths in the back corner. 'You can say it here.'

'Yeah,' Eddie nodded. 'But before we talk profit and loss, I gotta quality test. Not sure you're gonna want an audience.'

The fiery caroler began to sing again, but he was only as far as 'deck' before realizing his smaller friend had put on his coat and was preparing to leave. He coughed as though that would disguise his mistake, then followed suit. Sara watched as the two men stumbled over each other through the door. If she did what she was about to, she was sure she would see one or both of them again. But, still, she didn't want them to leave. They were the only people in the bar who hadn't heard her conversation with Eddie, which meant they were the only ones who didn't know how much was about to change. She stared at the door until it latched, sealing out the winter air and leaving Sara alone with Eddie, Steve, Angie, and the girl she was about to be.

'That's it then?' she said. 'It's fuck or nothing?'

'Whoa,' Eddie said. 'No one said fuck, Sweet Pea.'

'Wishful thinking,' Steve said.

'Could be,' Eddie said.

'So, she's leaving then.' The anger in Angie's voice was mixed with fear, like a child who couldn't admit their dare had gone too far.

'All these conclusions,' Eddie said. 'All the girls—jumping.'

His eyes traveled Sara's body, staring as though he hadn't before, discovering, not rediscovering, her breasts, waist, and legs. Sara had known this look since high school. Since puberty. Since sometimes before. Dark hair, light eyes. Strong but not threatening. Round but not soft. It was biology. Genetics. It was just her luck.

'It's like I've been saying for years. We give, they take,' Steve seemed to consider swinging his hips again but instead kept his body on his stool and his attention on his glass. 'That's nature,' he said, 'undeniable, and still the ladies get it wrong.'

'Maybe if y'all gave it right,' Angie said.

'Fuck off, Ang.'

She grabbed the drink from Steve's hands and poured it on the floor. 'You're done.'

'See? That's what I mean. You're the one that has to mop *and* the one dumping shit. Straight illogical.'

Eddie leaned close to Sara's ear, 'I'll be quick,' he whispered, almost kindly. He held out his hand.

Sara stood and followed Eddie. She wanted her mother there. She wanted all mothers there. She knew there were other people who could help her make this choice or at least help explain things in a way that made her choice okay. Tell her it was how much she needed and how little time she had. Tell her other people did it. People from here. Women that Eddie knew. She looked at Angie, but the bartender wouldn't meet her eyes. This was crazy, she thought. She was crazy. This couldn't be the way. She thought of the times in her past when she'd separated her body from the things she was doing with it. For protection. For denial. So, she could forget when it was over. That was it. Done. Sara thought of that morning. She thought of what she knew she had to do. She tried to add up the bills from the tops of the stacks and multiply that number by the amount she imagined from the bills she would never see. She told herself there was no other way. Not now. Not anymore. She smelled her own sweat and the old limes. She wanted someone to tell her this wasn't the way. She wondered if the vinyl on the bench seats would stick to her skin or if the lights in the back would deepen the shadows around Eddie's eyes. She wondered if Steve would pretend not to hear.

She thought I can do this. It'll only be a minute.

She thought—remember the coal dust. If she breathed it in, she could spit it out.

Thomas and Will
Felicity Reid

Anne, sixty and rotund like a well-ripened apple, waddles along the stone-flagged corridor towards her husband's office. He calls it that to give himself an air of importance she doesn't think he merits, but she's never argued the point. 'When I was in London…' he's wont to say, if ever she questions his foibles. As she's fed up with hearing that after three long years, she holds her tongue.

Retired. Huh. She's never heard the like. Her *own* father kept on working till the day he died, but *no*, working's too good for *her* husband. He likes to sprawl in his unbuttoned doublet and wrinkled hose, feet on his desk, pretending to be doing things that matter.

Not that what he did in London was *real* work. Even he had to admit that. 'It might make me money, Anne,' he's said, more than once. 'But I get paid for doing something I love. What could be better?'

Only now he's not doing it but getting under her feet whenever she turns around. Like the kitchen cat. The cook swears she keeps it for the vermin, but it's fat as butter, and *not* from eating mice. It's either asleep in front of the kitchen fire or slinking about the house in search of a corner to crap in. So, Anne has to keep all the bedroom doors closed.

She pauses outside the office. Will likes everyone to knock before they enter, and she raises her hand. But this is only so he can remove his booted feet from the desk and pretend to be doing something useful. The smell of tobacco smoke wafts under the door. He's at it again. Smoking and doing nothing.

Her hand drops, and she turns the handle.

Will is leaning back in his ornate chair, feet on the desk and a clay pipe clamped between his remaining teeth. Dirty, smelly habit. The pipe, not the feet on the desk. Why men have taken to it the way they have defeats her. Women, too, although not nearly so many, as it's also an *expensive* habit.

Will starts in guilty surprise. In a comical hurry, he whips his feet off the desk like a frightened schoolboy caught by the master in some mischief. 'My dear, I didn't hear you knock.'

Anne smoothes down her kirtle and bestows a taut smile on her husband. 'That's because I *didn't*.'

Will's eyes sharpen in interest. She doesn't often disturb his morning. 'What is it?'

'Judith.'

Will sighs. 'What does she want *this* time?'

Anne refrains from fiddling with the bunch of keys hanging from her waist. It irks her to have to go to Will every time she wants to help her daughter. Until three years ago, she could do as she liked with the money he sent from London. His return marked her demotion from household head to simple chattel. No wonder Judith, who'd been content to remain at home in their peaceful, all-female household, leapt at the first man who made an offer. And not many do that when you've already turned thirty.

It's this man who's the problem. She knows it, and Will knows it too.

'She feels we—*you're* elbowing her Thomas out. You don't consider him part of the family. She says you and Susanna's John go drinking all the time. And ignore Thomas.'

Will scowls, running a hand over his balding head as though smoothing non-existent hair down. 'Thomas owns an inn. What does he want to come drinking with John and me for?'

'That's not what she means.'

Will shrugs. 'Can I help not liking the man? His face would sour ripe grapes.'

As Anne doesn't like him either, she stays quiet.

Will continues, stoking himself up with dislike. 'He's a *fancy-monger*. The day after they married—*illegally*, I might add, as it was Shrovetide—he was up in the Consistory Court for getting another woman with child.' He leans forward, well into the swing of his diatribe. 'But what's done can't be undone. Hasty marriage seldom proveth well.'

Anne rises to Judith's defence. 'Stop quoting your poetry at me. Did you want her to end an old maid? Her sister's been teasing her for years that she'd never find a man fool enough to marry her. Could she help jumping at the first one who offered?'

Will snorts. 'Frailty, thy name is surely woman.'

Anne bristles. 'He hid his faults uncommon well, husband. You've said yourself that the devil can cite scriptures for his purpose.' She straightens her back. 'But that's all behind him now. Judith wants you to accept him into the family.' She cringes inside, for all Thomas has brought her beloved younger daughter so far is excommunication, and she fears things will only get worse.

Will huffs. 'Well…as it's my birthday…I *suppose* he could join John and myself, and a few of my friends. We'd thought to spend the night in celebration of my fifty years on this mortal coil.'

'Fifty-*two*.'

His eyes twinkle. 'If you say so.'

She allows herself a smile. If Will is going out drinking, again, with his London friends, then she'll get a peaceful night. If she's lucky, they could be gone until dawn. 'Shall I tell her?'

Will nods. 'What harm can it do?'

*

Thomas, Judith's husband for the past ten weeks, walks with a jaunty step, careful not to tread in anything noisesome in the dark. He mustn't spoil his fashionable new shoes whose huge rosettes match the clocks on his hose. He gives his short cloak a toss over his shoulder worthy of any London gentleman and fingers his sword hilt. An affectation for a vintner and tobacconist, but, nevertheless, necessary for the part he wants to play. After all, he's going to meet Will's sophisticated London friends tonight, and who knows but that they might introduce him to useful contacts.

At Will's house, opposite the Guild Chapel, Thomas approaches the arched gateway. Closed, of course, but he doesn't need to knock. He steps inside. He's been here before, but not in such auspicious circumstances. No, the last time, six weeks since, was to explain to Will why the Consistory Court had excommunicated him and Judith. An unpleasant interview.

But tonight, the excommunication no longer seems so bad, and he's heard it's soon to be brushed beneath the rug. And he's here by invitation. To celebrate Will's birthday. As though he *likes* the man.

He strides into the courtyard as if he owns it. One day, he will. Perhaps. Will only has two daughters, his son having died young, and Thomas is counting on half of everything his father-in-law owns. And that's *a lot*.

This is the biggest house in town, and the hall matches it, stretching taller than the two storeys of the service range.

Thomas steps through the doorway.

A hearth occupies one side of the hall, with a tall chimney to draw the smoke. It doesn't throw out much heat unless you're right in front of it. Will and his friends hog the heat, warming their backsides against the flames and holding flagons of mulled ale. Laughing. Perhaps at Thomas.

He knows John, Susanna's husband, the *favoured* son-in-law. A doctor and a puritan, the latter by lip-service only. Higher in the social rankings that a tavern owner, even if he calls himself a vintner. The look in John's and Will's eyes tells Thomas he'll always be a tavernkeeper to them.

But who are the others? Four men, all around Will's age or a little younger, with a reckless air about them, as though the world is theirs to do with as they wish. To take, to shape, to mould to their own device. None of them as well-dressed as Thomas. It's as though they've all thrown on the nearest doublet and jerkin and come rushing out, pell-mell.

Thomas meets Will's eyes, his cold, unwelcoming eyes, and regrets asking Judith to intercede. It's clear Will hasn't forgotten the illegal marriage, the dead bastard and the excommunication.

Well, Thomas won't stand for that. But he can wait. He can smile and smile at these casual ne-er-do-wells with their unbuttoned jerkins, their slashed sleeves and untidy hair.

Will's mouth smiles, but his eyes don't. 'Ah, Thomas. Come and meet my friends, all down from London for my birthday.'

No one has ever travelled miles to see Thomas. He approaches the group, on the outside looking in. 'Good evening, gentlemen.' Only they're not gentlemen at all. Not really. They're near as bad as whorehouse owners. What's Susanna's John doing mixing with them? What's he thinking of? Arse-licking Will, that's what. Insinuating himself amongst Will's dissipate friends. Slithering into the family fold.

'This is Ben, Michael, Henry and Richard. You know John already, of course. My friends, this is Judith's husband, Thomas.' Will sounds pissed already.

Richard, a short, stout fellow, with cheeks and nose reddened by broken veins, is already full of ale-induced bonhomie. 'Thomas, my boy. Welcome. Will said he'd got Judith off his hands at last. Let me pour you a tankard of ale.'

He throws an arm around Thomas's shoulders and heads him to where a jug of ale stands with a poker heating it.

Henry, whose round, unlined face is reminiscent of an adult baby, is already there pouring himself a refill. 'We're off out shortly,' he says, as jovial as Richard. 'Will says you own a tavern? My God, man, that's heaven on Earth. My vote's to start there.'

Ben drains his tankard. 'Let's go, now we're all assembled. I feel a need to take a likely wench upon my knee and buss her.'

'You always feel a need for that,' scoffs Michael, whose grey hair marks him as the oldest of the group and possibly the most responsible. 'I've never known you not.'

John laughs, a deep, throaty guffaw, so unlike his normal persona that Thomas stares at him. Prim Susanna wouldn't recognise her husband. Thomas wonders if he'll be able to buss a comely wench or two himself. Less sour-faced ones than his wife, who's not yet forgiven him the stigma of their excommunication.

'Come, let's go.' Richard's voice is deep and melodious, as though accustomed to declaiming to a crowd. 'I would give all my fame for a pot of ale.'

They surge into the chilly courtyard where a maid is by the well. No sign of Anne.

Ben lunges at the serving girl. 'Give us a kiss, my pretty. I have a fair thought to lie between maids' legs.'

Will drags him away. 'Not on *my* doorstep you don't. Come on.'

Thomas follows the group, still observing rather than participating. They stagger, because they've all drunk a lot of ale before even setting out, heading towards the water meadows. This is territory Thomas knows well. They're heading for his tavern. Atwood's. Everything they drink will put money in his pocket.

Not so. 'On the house, I think you said, Thomas?' shouts Will above the general hubbub. And Thomas can't demur, or he'll look mean. He grits his teeth and orders ale for Will's party, glad they've already half-filled themselves at home.

They find a table and Thomas squeezes in on a corner, an afterthought on the enjoyment of their night.

'Let's drink to success!' cries Richard, swinging his tankard of Thomas's best ale above his head. 'Long life and success to us all!'

Tankards smash together.

'Long life and success!'

Thomas joins in, without much enthusiasm.

'What're you working on now, Will?' asks Ben.

Are they in the same line of business as Will? Probably. They have that look about them. As though they see themselves as a cut above men like Thomas, who have to work for a living. What *they* do isn't work. But at least, unlike in some families, there are only two children to share Will's wealth. When Judith gets her share, he, Thomas, as her husband, will control it. As he lies in bed at nights, since even before he married Judith, he's been spending what he sees as his own inheritance.

'Oh, just my accounts and investments,' answers Will, draining his flagon of ale. 'I've put aside all other activities with my retirement.'

Michael slaps Will on the back. 'You lie, good friend. I can't believe that you, the best of us, have laid your quill down, never to take it up again.'

Ben makes a grab for the girl bringing more ale, pulling her into his lap.

'*My bounty is as boundless as the sea,*
My love as deep. The more I give to thee,
The more I have, for both are infinite.'

The girl gives a cackle of laughter that grates on Thomas's ears. Did Judith for one moment suspect her father's birthday celebrations would be like this?

'You thief!' shouts Will. '*I* wrote that!'

'Then you should be flattered,' cries Richard. 'Your lines are most appropriate, and plainly our talentless friend Ben could think of nothing better to say.'

The girl wriggles free. 'I got work to do.' He slaps her on her behind as she flounces away, her laughter carrying above the rumble of men's voices.

They down their ale faster than Thomas has ever seen anyone down ale. In quantities larger than any he's seen before, as well. No doubt all the quicker because it's costing them nothing.

Thomas's fingers feel the concealed pocket he had inserted by the seamstress who made it. Always good to keep a few coins in, and, right now, the Inheritance Powder he purchased from that travelling barber surgeon two months since. It's been in there waiting for just such an occasion as this.

They're talking about London now. Even John, who's never been there in his life, is joining in as though he's part of their clique. A club for those in the know. Well, none of them are in the know, did they but realise.

'I'll get us some refills,' Thomas says, gathering their empty tankards. They pay him no attention as he heads off to the bar. Too busy boasting about all the performances they've done at court over the winter. Trying to make Will miss his old life.

The man behind the bar, Jem Rutledge, gives Thomas a raised eyebrow as he fills the tankards yet again. Thomas takes four back for Ben, Michael, Henry and Richard. The next three are for himself, John and Will, When Jem turns away to another customer, Thomas sprinkles his long-hoarded Inheritance Powder into Will's tankard and swirls it with a hasty finger.

He mustn't mistake which one is Will's, although he wouldn't be sorry to say goodbye to two-faced John, public puritan and private drunk. He hands out the ale. Richard, redder in the face than ever, proposes another toast. 'To life and love, to a warm woman in a soft bed, or a soft woman in a warm bed, and to our good friend Will. May we all be back here on St George's Day in *another* fifty years.'

They down their ale like water. Will bangs his empty tankard down and wipes his mouth on his sleeve.

Thomas's work is done. 'I think I might head off to bed,' he says to no one in particular. 'I've had more to drink than I'm used to. I'll leave you to enjoy the night.'

No one even says goodnight.

Thomas skips up the stairs to the rooms he and Judith share above the tavern.

*

He barely sleeps. His stomach churns and his heart pounds fit to burst. After breaking his fast with Judith, he suggests they might walk round to her parents' house. 'I think I might have left one of my gloves in the hall.'

They find the house in turmoil.

John is upstairs in Will's chamber with Anne.

Susanna, exuding daughterly concern, is there too, clutching her child's hand. 'Father's caught a chill,' she tells Judith. 'His throat's sore, and he's shaking and been sick. He says his belly pains him and his heart pounds.'

Wide-eyed, the child shrinks against her mother's skirts; the only offspring Susanna and John have managed to raise past infancy.

Time ticks past.

Judith strides up and down.

Susanna wrings her hands.

Thomas takes the heavy master's chair by the cold hearth. Yes. *This* is where he'll sit when all of this is his. He'll lay claim to this house as part of his and Judith's share. Back in January, when he asked Judith to marry him, Will made the mistake of showing him the will he'd just had witnessed. 'I want to ensure both my girls are taken care of, so I've made ample provision for both of them, you'll see. Half each.'

It was the showing of that will that sealed his new father-in-law's fate and had Thomas inveigling Judith into marrying in haste during the forbidden Shrovetide. That, and the mounting debts, and collectors who don't care that you can't work if you have broken arms and legs, drove him on.

Now he's reached the summit of his ambition, and all will be well.

At last, John comes downstairs, each tread creaking beneath his weight. He shakes his head, tears in his eyes.

Susanna wails.

Judith stops her pacing.

Thomas sits very still. In the house that is now his.

*

Will Shakespeare is six feet under when the will is read.

It's been changed.

Judith, and it *is* Judith, not Thomas, gets three hundred pounds as her marriage portion.

Susanna gets everything else.

Judith regards Thomas out of eyes as cold as her father's. 'He changed his will a month ago. Because of *you*. John told me. He didn't want *you* getting your hands on a penny of it, not after the scandal of that woman and her brat.'

Thomas's chest is hollow with fear as his fingers stray unbidden to his concealed pocket and the screw of paper that once held the powders.

Hoist with his own petard, as Will would say.

2023 CYGNATURE SHORT STORY PRIZE WINNER

Cygnature Short Story Prize Judge
J S Watts

I was extremely pleased to have been asked to judge the 2023 Cygnature Story Prize and enjoyed reading the diverse pieces submitted by the youthful—well, youthful in relation to me— entrants who submitted their work.

I was impressed by the originality of a great many of the stories and the wide range they encompassed.

With such a diverse spread of offerings, I felt the need to be equally broad and open in terms of what I was seeking from the most successful stories. I was about to write that I approached judging from both a writer's and a reader's perspective, but although there may be slightly nuanced differences, ultimately, I think they are largely one and the same.

The writer in me was looking for strong technique and well-edited work: structure, narrative development, style, sound punctuation, grammar and spelling, and purposeful use of point of view. The reader was looking for something striking that reached out and grabbed my attention, absorbed me within its narrative and made me want to read on. This reader, however, was not going to be grabbed if she kept stumbling over poorly edited work that was grammatically incorrect and clunky. Nor was the writer going to fall in love with a story, however technically perfect, if there wasn't an emotional or intellectual connection with the tale being told. If truth be told, the writer also wanted to find a story she wished she'd written herself, whereas the reader just wanted a good, enjoyable read, but they were permitted some individuality.

I should probably admit that, in addition to the reader and the writer, my complicated judging persona also contained an editor. What the editor was looking for was simply a story she would enthusiastically and unhesitatingly publish in any of the anthologies and magazines she has been involved with.

To simplify things, as far as a complex trio of personalities can, what the reader, editor and writer were ultimately looking for was sound writing-craft and an original, engaging read.

I found all of the above in *One Last Dream,* an Africa-based story about the last White Rhino, her devoted guardian keeper, and the joy that can be found even in the bleakest of situations. Its ecological focus was relevant and contemporary. The story telling managed to be both simple and complex, brutal and gently emotional, and it made me cry.

I acknowledge that enjoyment of a story is a personal thing and necessarily subjective. What one reader responds to, another doesn't. Think about it. How many times have you enjoyed a book that a close friend or family member has not? Nevertheless, a story that makes a reader cry has succeeded in creating a moment that is real enough to draw the reader in so deeply that it allows them to believe in the emotions it has generated – no mean feat.

Other stories that I felt deserved an honourable mention were *Sungazing, Mischief, Confessions to Mrs. Dalloway Through a Bathroom Door* and *The Ballad of Small Beginnings.* Each demonstrated different strengths: strong style and characterization, a humorous and entertaining approach to the fantasy genre, stylish literary resonance with human insight, writing on multiple levels and a dryly humorous, intellectually entertaining fable.

If the above serves as a summary of what I was looking for and what engaged me most, I would be remiss if I didn't comment about the many other stories I read. Just because I haven't mentioned them by title, doesn't mean I didn't enjoy reading them.

I was struck by the originality of the stories and their wide range of subject matter. Works encompassed dragons, the Death of gods, more mundane murderers, lovers, a bodiless child (well, actually just his head) who sparks a rebellion, people going about their daily business, people discovering their sexuality, refugees seeking a better life, a modern Icarus and a young man optimistically going off to fight in World War One.

There were some interesting, focused pieces that I would define more as vignettes or monologues than stories. However well-crafted for that style of writing, they ultimately didn't make it to my short list, because of a lack of narrative progression or character development. I was looking for stories with plot and/ or character evolution that moved forward in some way from where they began.

Sadly, some stories broke my focus, and therefore my engagement as a reader, because of overt weaknesses in technique, specifically the number of typos, grammatical bloopers and word misuse they contained. The writer part of my psyche wanted to advise rigorous and repeated editing of a piece before submission. Editing, that is, that involves more than a quick application of a spell-checker programme. I'll freely admit to being a compulsive editor of my own work (and, yes, despite that, I do still miss typos), but, brushing aside my own obsession, the process of editing should lead to a polished piece of writing that will shine and attract a reader's attention, as opposed to snagging them on the roughness of its craft. I guess you could call these stories diamonds in the rough, with lots of potential that had yet to be revealed by clearing away unwanted debris.

If the above seems a little harsh, given that this is a competition for young writers relatively new to their craft, then all I will say is that the best stories I came across could have been written by a professional writer of any age or maturity. I willingly admit that I judged all the stories submitted against the standards set by the best and the best were very good.

One Last Dream
Daniel Key

Obuya was always disappointed to see a stranger through his scope. It meant he had met another person who would sully his opinion of the world.

After he would step over their bodies, searching through their things, he always found notes of money and jangling change. Shotguns or rifles they could sell, clothes on their back they could swap for food in their stomach. But here they were, hunting after Nasima, the only northern white rhino still walking the earth.

It seemed as though every day Obuya had to defend Nasima from a new poacher eager for her horn. Aren't we all siblings? He thought. Doesn't hurting her hurt you?

Riches talk, though, riches whisper false promises into the poor man's ear. Imagine a world in which you'd never be hungry, the riches whisper. Imagine a world in which you could have whatever you want.

Obuya had been Nasima's guardian for the last six years, following her day and night from before she became the last living of her kind. She had a friend, Nesari. They were the last two on this earth. Obuya would lie with Nasima, resting his palm on her broad side, stroking her rough, grey skin, and she would lay there beside him and sleep, her mind filled with bright dreams and overwhelming love. Obuya had long decided that rhinos could dream. He'd spent far too long by her side as she was floating through the unconscious world to think otherwise. Sometimes she would kick in her sleep or let out a breath of air so covered in joy that it was impossible for Obuya not to smile. She must've been dreaming of the past, days in the company of her brethren and her sisters. He would look up at the clear night's sky and wonder if she ever looked up at the stars in reverence like he did, if she considered the world as beautiful or just accepted it how it was. He wondered if she ever got sad, if she could tell through some intuition that it all ends with her. That after she passes the world is deprived of something unique, and everything moves one step closer to being the same.

The team on Nasima was much larger than just Obuya, but each rhino had a personal guardian assigned to them. Someone trustworthy and clean-hearted, with a record unsoiled by corruption, and, most importantly, someone more stubborn than a rhino's hide.

Nasima had fifteen men on her at all times. Obuya in her immediate vicinity, with at least two team members with eyes on her, then two more patrolling the immediate perimeter of around two hundred metres. All the rest patrolled the general vicinity of the reservation.

On occasion, Obuya would run his hand over Nasima's precious horn. Hard as granite, but so perfectly smooth. The only reason she couldn't live a true life. Something as silly as a horn. One hundred thousand dollars per kilo. That was the price of the precious weapon he held in his hand. That was what the price used to be, anyway. Now that this was the final one, he imagined the price would be much greater. The rarer the gem the more a collector will pay.

*

Obuya's team found Nesari dead three years ago. The team protecting her was found slaughtered in the vicinity of her corpse. She was lying down with her head resting in the dirt, her body all rough grey apart from the stumps where the horns used to be. Those two holes were bright red, violently cut so that every inch of horn was taken. Her body lay mutilated and lifeless. A rough charcoal carpet of a pelt and rancid meat too disgusting for any man to eat. The hornless creature would never dream again.

The hope for population growth had extinguished by then, of course. Two rhinos left, but both female. The last male had perished years before that. Critically endangered now being only a mark of pity. The northern white rhino was extinct, it just hadn't happened yet. Obuya had heard talk and declaration of prophecy his entire life, but this was the only one he watched with his own eyes, it was the only one he ever believed in.

There was a prophecy bestowed on him once when he was a child. His aunt was the one who made the claim.

'You will witness the beginning of the Rapture,' she declared.

Being only a boy, Obuya was quick to brush off her words, especially given her previous predictions. Once, an old woman who she had determined was to die in a fortnight went on living until she passed a century of life.

But still, he remembered the words, and thought about them from time to time, wondering if a rapture would ever come.

Nasima and he would sleep next to one another. Nasima lying on her stomach facing north whilst Obuya would be propped up on her side, resting his back against her. He would fall asleep watching the stars dancing in the sky above.

*

One day, there was a commotion far off in the distance on the plains. Not poachers letting off shots, but two giraffes locked in battle, cracking bone on bone with every whip of their necks. Obuya was used to this sight. It always reminded him of fights he'd seen people have over women. The giraffes, with their long necks and blue tongues, standing tree high. The men with their fists clenched and their eyes full of rage. Entertainment, Obuya thought. There's entertainment everywhere in the wild.

He turned to Nasima, wondering if she was entertained, then frowned his eyebrow at her. She was watching the battle in the distance. But was tilted slightly, watching from a diagonal. There was no grass for her to graze on, and no distraction to partake in. He approached his friend from the side she had turned away from the action. He rubbed her hide, and she jumped a little, turning the whole of her body to face him. Incessant flies buzzing around her one good eye.

Obuya was sure that the dreams of the blind were more vivid than those blessed with sight. That was the saving grace of bearing such an affliction. If all a person could see existed in their dreams, then surely they must brighten and take flight amongst the ever-present darkness they saw. Nasima must be having brighter dreams than every other soul sitting underneath the starry sky overlooking Laikipia.

From that day on, Obuya made sure to stay at Nasima's right side, so she could always see him inside the tightened cone of her world. If she had anything she had him, at least. She was also, Obuya thought one night, the closest thing this world has to unique. One of one and never to be seen again. A single star in a universe of darkness. A single bird gliding over the ocean. The final witness.

*

Poachers are men possessed. The object of their desires is Orion's star, their guiding starlight. The world exists around it and nothing else matters.

Some are bold, moving with violence brewing in their palms, letting off gunfire with glee, thinking they could kill the entirety of their guard on their own. These men are rare but not extinct. Delusions are popular amongst people whose god is a growth of bone. Most of them, aren't like that, though.

Obuya had stopped counting. The number was beginning to scare him. Occasionally he wondered how many more he'd have to kill before there weren't any left. He reserved himself to accept the sad truth that they would never stop. Only Nasima's death would stop anything.

*

It was three weeks since he'd found out about Nasima's blindness when another poacher wandered into the reserve hoping God would aid him in achieving his dreams.

Wambua slipped past the first set of patrolling guards under the cover of night, hiding amongst the patches of bush and underneath the low-hanging leaves of the trees scattered across the plains. His friend sitting in a pickup truck at the meeting point, and two more friends in a car waiting for the right moment.

Once the guards went to do their rounds once more, the poacher slipped past them. Getting closer and closer towards his prize.

Obuya was sitting with his friend, a hand resting on her body, his eyes gazing up at the stars. It was a bright, clear night, illuminated by starfall. Nasima was sound asleep, dreaming.

Wambua approached without sound, masking the rustling of the grass he ran through with the sounds of the wind.

Gunfire in the distance. He peered out from the bushes at four Jeeps rushing to the sounds to extinguish the threat. Once they were gone and the sounds of gunfire erupted and illuminated the night in a cacophony of rapture, Wambua sprinted in the direction the Jeeps had appeared from.

Obuya held his rifle in one hand and left his other resting on Nasima. Her dream extinguished, pulled back to the world to witness the sounds of death. Obuya was drowning in adrenaline, his heart pumping lightning. Every sense available to him heightened beyond human levels of perception. The eyes of a leopard and the nose of a hyena, the ears of an antelope. And those other senses vibrating alive with the lightning. He felt, in the single moment they fell upon him, the eyes of a stranger peering at him from the darkness and he lit up the evil with bullets whose shells rattled as they fell onto the ground.

Nasima was up and whining at the racket but calmed by Obuya's returning hand and soothing whispers.

'Backup, backup,' he shot into his radio in between the whispers.

He never saw Wambua's body, but he knew it was there by the thud made when it was deposited into the bed of a pickup truck and driven away.

Nasima was back asleep, lost in her dreams. Obuya did not sleep that night, but he stayed with her. He made sure his friend was dreaming something sweet.

*

A year passed. More attempts, more failures. Nasima started to lose sight in her right eye, and the doctors were assuming she was going deaf as well. Forty-eight years she'd lived. Only four rhinos in captivity had ever passed fifty. None of them had gone blind.

Obuya could feel the energy of his friend sapping away as the days went on. She was sleeping more and more. Eating less. He wondered how the world looked with nothing inside it.

Then the day came when he woke from his sleep not propped on her back but flat on the floor, looking into the early morning sky so blue it was green. He sat up and looked around. The plains were clear. He couldn't see a single patrol, couldn't hear the engine of a Jeep. No animals on the horizon, no clouds in the sky. It was Obuya alone in the world.

'Nasima? Where are you?' he asked to the wind. But the wind answers to no man.

'Nasima? he shouted as he ran around the reserve. He asked the trees, and he asked the bushes, and he asked the grass.

A flock of birds flew overhead, and he asked them. He asked the wandering antelope, and he asked a strolling water-buffalo, and he asked the endless sky.

A Jeep came by, and he signalled it over.

'Where's Nasima?' he asked.

'Didn't you hear?' the guard asked back.

'Hear what?'

'You stayed asleep this whole time?' The guard laughed. 'They should fire you; a guardian who doesn't know where his animal is.'

'Where is she?' Obuya asked, one last time.

'The watering-hole. She's still there. Hop on.'

Obuya stood inside the Jeep, with his arms resting against the roof, gazing off into the distance. Nasima hadn't visited the watering hole in three years.

'How did you know to take her there?' he asked.

'We didn't. She took us and we followed.'

'But she's blind,' Obuya said.

'She has a good memory,' the guard said, tapping his index to his forehead.

The watering hole came into view. Usually dense with creatures, on that morning it was empty. Obuya couldn't see Nasima there either. He was about to ask the guard again when he spotted movement. Inside the shallow watering hole, Nasima was splashing around and decorating the land in sparkles of water, moving with a vigour and grace Obuya hadn't seen from her in years.

The Jeep pulled up and Obuya ran out towards the water. Nasima looked up at the noise, seizing up for a moment, but somehow, she knew it was Obuya running towards her, she could feel it in her heart where she couldn't see it in her eyes. And her whole person lit up as she recognised her greatest friend. Obuya jumped inside the water with her, cascading manmade rain down on the plains. The two of them ran around in the water, playing like children in a never-ending dream.

2023 BEDFORD SHORT STORY PRIZE WINNER

Bedford Short Story Prize Judge's Report
Paul Barnes

The more I read short stories—especially those that have not the rigour of editing for formal publication—the more I realise that there is a very fine line between doing too much or too little with the language. There must be some spark that makes the reader glad to have read it, and the writer glad to have written, but grab too much into the short space of the narrative, and the action or ambition can overwhelm the dimensions of the tale.

Whether it is my 1982 reading of D R Barnes (no relation) editing *Short Stories of Our Time,* where readers require 'relevance to them and a relationship with the reality that they know'; or whether it is my 2023 re-reading of Hilary Mantel's 2014 collection *The Assassination of Margaret Thatcher* (there was such mayhem going on in 2023) with her 'scalpel-sharp observation and a prodigal gift for imagery', as Maggie Gee wrote on the back cover, there has to be neither too much action and passion nor too little creativity and impulse.

Some of the fifteen stories I have had the privilege of reading were determined to be in the decade of X (formerly Twitter) and lost sight of readability.

Few stories were geographically specific, but one exception told of a ship's captain's suicide in the south China seas. Maybe elsewhere it was suicide when the birdwatcher's too chatty lady went for a swim and apparently drowned. Accident perhaps, but the tale is about his perception, his greater concern for the birds and nature. There was a good deal of apocalypse: Fred and his narrator were in love during Armageddon in a bunker; Plato and other philosophy rubbed against jazz and recognisable life before the bunker. Elsewhere, replace Lucius with Ulysses, and you have a positively classical story with an overlay of *Pirates of the Caribbean,* as his ship is chased into the foggy jungle estuary by Harlen Veech.

Grief was, perhaps, the most common emotion. The top potato farmer scatters father's ashes, amid fears of the succession and of the birds. A narrator lost an aged mother, and cared for ageing father, whose "Grief is a kind of madness." An agoraphobic son goes to buy a suitable floral gift for his mother, the twist being he is to put it on her grave. Another story told of "Grief's gift of creative impotence [which] was bestowed upon me with little warning", as a bereaved musician purchases a house with what turns out to be a marvellous prototype organ.

Among the other candidates, *Headland* was remarkably topical, a compact tale of a (Hemsby-style) house and woman on the edge of crumbling cliff and crumbling life. Clever levels of parallel lives—the gull, the mirror…[I read this on the day a huge landslide on the Isle of Wight saw around twenty homes evacuated just two weeks before Christmas.] The dispassionate insights and economy make this my runner-up story.

The Truffle Hunters wins my award for another post-apocalypse story (red fields, yellow sky, hiding in holes and ruined buildings; some in castles). Voynich and his deaf mutant sow Pod seek for truffles for the castle-dwellers, defying threats from people with dogs; helped by Hare ('them'), evidently a rare piece of compassion across classes in a disturbed society, with a quiet forgiving ending. Something of *The Road* here. As in our terms truffle is one of the most expensive foods, it is favoured by the castle-dwellers, and thus a key item in the economy. It is not only Mantel who has a gift for imagery.

The Truffle Hunters
Lucia Wilde

They emerge from the burrow to a bloody sunset, and the hare. Stood frozen, mad eyes very wide. Sighted.

Then Pod snorts, nudging Voynich's legs, and the hare streaks off across red doused fields. He exhales slowly and starts walking. It isn't an omen. Just an animal that knows better than to linger. Pod's tail flicks from side to side as she trots ahead. She's happy to be out and it makes Voynich smile, lengthening his stride to catch up with her. Not that she'd ever leave him behind, glancing back every few metres to check he's still there.

(The castle agent had called her 'unlovely' as if Voynich had cared to know his opinion on an earless runt of a sow, as if it mattered, as if Voynich would suddenly realise he didn't want a pallid, round-headed mutant creature. Pod was his. No one was queuing up to offer him a better animal that didn't burn in the sun and shiver in the cold. He wouldn't have wanted one if they were.)

Out of sight of the burrow and into the trees, Pod stops and waits for Voynich to unbuckle her harness. He makes sure to scratch the skin the straps covered for her as she rumbles in relief. Pigs are supposed to be harnessed and leashed at all times out of doors, but Pod hates it and she's never run off. Never been more than a few feet from Voynich's side in her whole life.

They walk on together in the long sunset with Voynich leaning on his stick and Pod snuffling. Too close to home to really find anything not uncovered by the others in the daylight but Voynich thinks it's the search she enjoys. Mist creeps over the leaf litter and between the straight trunks, lit up by the dying light, everything pink and gold.

Pod picks their path. Toward the ruins this time. Dangerous to go too close but the pig knows things a man can't. Voynich trusts her.

She stops by a hornbeam at the edge of the stone garden and digs, snout working, until Voynich helps with his stick and trowel. He's careful for the last bit, brushing earth away to uncover her prize. A good-sized black truffle. Voynich beams and plants a kiss on that muddy snout. Pod gets an apple slice to whuffle down as he tucks the truffle away. That alone has made the evening worth it, but they've barely started yet.

Pod trots onwards with no care paid to the tilted or broken slabs of stone around them. Voynich peers past the moss and lichens at the unknowable letters, words.

What was important enough to carve into stone and leave standing here for eternity?

Not that Pod knows, or cares, pausing to look back at Voynich until he hurries up to join her at the hollowed shell of a building. It must have been grand once. Stone too, carved blocks of it, broken figures and ornate windows. The tree roots break through the worn slabs of the floor and their branches reach for the sky where there was once roof.

With Pod snuffling around the trees and broken-down walls, Voynich stands in the cross section, the middle of what it used to be, head tilted back to watch light and shadow play on stone.

He closes his eyes and listens.

Somewhere far away people sing. Lots of them, high and ethereal, like Voynich imagines ghosts would. Maybe there are ghosts here. It's not a hostile place though. Not a sad place. A peaceful one.

Pod nudges against his legs and turns her snout up into his hand. He scratches her head, and she moves on and out, knowing he'll follow. Down the hill they find a smaller couple of truffles beneath a young ash. Pod is well pleased with her apple slices. They stop by the pond so she can drink and Voynich can crouch to squint into the murky depths. It's too dark to see anything. Sometimes there are great golden fish that can be good to eat, if you cook them right.

Birds argue in the birches as pig and man pass beneath, roosted and settling for the night, heedless of anything below. Pod's trotters click on old, broken tarmac. Voynich wonders if she knows this is risky. Forbidden. They're almost in the ruins proper.

Eyeless houses with jutting beams and rusted nothings abandoned outside. Twisted gates with what used to be an eagle carved in. Half a red pillar with a slot in it, innards open.

Another truffle under a half fallen down birch and a squirrel that watches as they dig. It's quiet.

They'll go to the river, if that's what Pod wants, decides Voynich. The river and back.

There's a distant thrumming in the sky to the south and the glittering lights of a castle. It moves so slowly you could barely say it does at all, hanging there, laughter carrying to Voynich on the cold wind. Maybe he imagines it. It's a world he's never seen and never will see but works to enrich. The truffles in his pouch will be in a place like that by weeks end. They still need them, up in the castles.

*

Pod shoves her head in an abandoned barrel and startles a cat. The brindled creature hisses and scrabbles into one of the ruined buildings, something clattering in the dark. Pod must have scented it. Been curious. Voynich lays a hand on her back to reassure her.

Disturbed dust swirls around them as they pass through the most dense part of the ruins. Exposed cables twist, broken glass crunches, a can rolls along mournfully. Voynich can hear the singing again, but here it's sad. This isn't a peaceful place. It's where the ghosts should be.

The light dies as they reach the river. The bridge is intact, if a little cracked and crumbling. They could cross if they wanted. Pod doesn't want, and Voynich is glad. He's never been that far. Instead, they wander along an old path and Pod finds him another truffle from one of the old planes that tower over blank ruins. He relies more on the stick to feel his way around obstacles.

Pod decides to sit at the water's edge for a little while and Voynich joins her to share the last half of the apple before they go back.

She can't have noticed the silence like Voynich does, but Pod freezes all the same. Does she hear the singing inside her head even though she's got no ears? Voynich isn't always convinced it comes to him by way of his own ears, so it would make sense.

That doesn't matter now.

It's stopped and Pod is so still.

She lurches up as a howl cuts the dark. Voynich finds himself on his feet too with terror flashing through him.

Barks follow hollowly. Hungrily.

A real laugh.

Voynich looks at Pod. There isn't time to harness her. He'll need to trust in her ability to follow him.

He takes off running, not as swift as the hare was, relying on his stick. It's too dark for this.

They're both graceless.

Blood pounds in Voynich's ears, thudding with his feet on broken concrete. He dares a glance and sees a flash of pale pink by his side. Pod is keeping up.

Something snarls.

Pod squeals. A horrible noise. One she rarely ever makes. She can smell them. She's scared.

So is Voynich.

A dark building rises ahead and then light.

Flickering. A doorway. Are they trapped? Caught between?

There's a shadow against the light, a person, and Pod runs for them. Voynich can't call to her, can't tell her that people doesn't always mean safe. She won't hear him. He has to follow, putting on speed, reaching for Pod but there's nothing to grab. No harness.

They both tumble through the doorway and it snaps shut behind them. The dogs bark, but outside. The dogs' people growl.

Pod has skidded to a halt in the unfamiliar space, some kind of passageway, leading into dark. She sniffs.

Voynich doubles over to drag in stale air and clasps his stick.

The figure peers between man and pig with their head tilted. Voynich finally gets a good look. Small, grubby, bundled up. Cropped dark hair and weathered skin. Not old. Big eyes that are very gold in this light. Wrapped in a blanket poncho and furs.

No dog.

They might not be safe yet, but this is an improvement.

'Thanks...' mumbles Voynich, head ducked.

'No problem,' answers the golden-eyed saviour. They let Pod sniff them and begin to smile, if reluctantly. 'Why's your pig got no ears?'

Voynich shrugs. 'Born like it.'

'S'cute. Come on. They'll not break the door down, they know better. But they'll lurk.' They jerk a thumb back at the door and scoop up that lantern to lead the way down the passageway. And it is down, if slowly. A ramp.

Pod keeps close to Voynich but she's not as fearful as he is. He starts to hear the sounds of people. Talk and cooking. Children playing. Through another door to a big, big room. The ceiling is lost in darkness. There are more lanterns, more than the burrow has. Gas bottles by the stoves.

And there's the wall. One massive wall that's covered in…in pictures? But moving ones. Flickering ones. Voynich stares. People in weird clothes do things he doesn't understand in bright daylight, under a blue sky. He'd heard the sky was supposed to be blue once.

Pod is staring too.

Their saviour realises they aren't following anymore and turns to look back with a knowing smirk.

'Come and sit,' they say, waking Voynich from his reverie. He nudges Pod and they both get moving again.

The others watch as they pass and Voynich feels conspicuous in his blue coat. The truffle hunters all wear blue, because the pigs can see it, but it has always felt like a lot when most of the other groups wear whatever they can find or make. Which is usually brown and grey. The blue cloth comes from the castles.

But these people have power and gas so they can't be badly off. They must have a relationship with the castles.

Voynich keeps his head down and Pod close.

They're taken to sit near one of the stoves, on floor cushions, and a hot drink is pressed into Voynich's hands by another indeterminate person in grey. Their saviour finds a bowl of scraps for Pod, who leans against Voynich as she eats.

'My name is Hare, by the way,' says the saviour.

Hare.

Voynich stares at them.

He realises he's being rude.

'Ah, I…I'm Voynich. This is Pod. Thank you, Hare. For saving us. And the hospitality. We…owe you.'

Hare smiles and sits too, peering at Voynich. 'You do. But it's not urgent. Wasn't going to hide and listen to the dogs crunching your bones.'

'What is this place?' asks Voynich, forgetting his manners again, but Hare doesn't seem to mind.

'The Pictures,' they say, the flickering light of the big wall playing over their face. 'And our home.'

Voynich shuffles so he can see the wall and Hare both. The strange people up there are dancing now, in such bright clothes as it almost hurts to look at.

Several children, well bundled in blankets, shuffle closer to Pod. She lies down to show she's gentle and they swarm to pat her with soft giggles.

'Why are you down here at night?' asks Hare. 'You have to know it isn't safe.'

'Pod's got sensitive skin. She burns in the sun. And she wanted to come down here. I tend to let her lead the way. Trust her.'

Voynich refuses to feel self-conscious or stupid about that. Dogs can come out of nowhere. Even in the day.

Hare stares at him incredulously, but it's not like they need to say anything more. Obviously, the truffle hunter is mad.

Voynich is used to people looking at him like that. So he just shrugs and sips his hot drink. It's good. Hot and sweet with a burn of something stronger.

'Right…' mutters Hare. 'Well. You can both stay in here until dawn and then I'll walk you back up to the park.'

'Thank you. You're very kind.'

'I know,' they say. 'Don't let the pig do her business anywhere. Unless she can do it in a bucket.'

They move off to speak to the old woman, and then others, leaving Voynich to answer childish questions about Pod, and where he's from, and what it's like being a truffle hunter, and does he really live under the ground in a big burrow?

Eventually the children are taken to beds behind curtains at the back of the big room but the images on the wall never stop. They change, a lot, and most of the adults keep half an eye on them. Some make notes about what they see.

Voynich leans back against Pod to watch until he slides away into sleep with shapes dancing in his mind and the sounds that go with the pictures playing only for him.

He dreams the stories they tell.

Dancing and singing in a smart black suit.

Standing, bereft, in the rain as his lover walks away from him.

Digging graves in the darkness.

Flying up in the blue sky in some roaring metal machine.

Gunning down the people that want to hurt him.

Riding a white horse by an endless expanse of water.Hare shakes his shoulder to wake him. There's a beam of light cutting through the quiet dark of the room from some distant crack in the roof. It sounds like most of the others are asleep. Pod is awake, but she hasn't moved yet. Apparently, content.

Voynich sits up and eats the strange kind of flapjack that gets pressed into his hand. He drinks purified water as Hare pulls on a scratched-up leather jacket and hides knives in their sleeves.

He thinks he probably likes Hare. And imagines they like him. They do smile at him a few times as he finishes his food and rises to go and wash his cups in one of the buckets for the purpose.

Pod is allowed at the scraps again before Hare leads them out and up into the late dawn.

The dust beyond the door has been disturbed in the night, as if something twisted and fought there, turned on itself. Voynich hears snarling without his ears.

Pod doesn't seem worried.

Hare takes them back the way they came the previous evening but keeps to the shade. Voynich wonders why, until he realises they're being mindful of Pod's skin. He's unspeakably grateful. He glances at the sky and tries to imagine it blue, like in the pictures. It stays stubbornly yellow.

They don't talk. Voynich isn't good at it, and Hare doesn't seem inclined. Pod couldn't hear them even if they did.

Voynich wasn't sure what Hare meant when they said the park, but it turns out to be the fields with the pond and golden fish. They pause by it and turn to him.

'There. You'll be safe from here; dogs prefer the ruins.'

Voynich ducks his head again. 'Thank you. You're welcome in the burrow if you ever get up that far. We're beyond the stone garden at the top of the hill. Through the trees.'

He chews his lip as Hare considers him, then digs into his pockets and comes out with a conker. It's very near perfect, oily smooth, deep copper highlights in the surface and very round. Found a few nights ago and treasured but he owes Hare something. More than this, really, but what else could he give?

He offers it to Hare, feeling his cheeks heat up.

It's a long moment until Hare takes the conker and tilts their head to study it, cradled in both grubby hands.

'You found this?' they ask, rubbing their thumb over the soft surface.

Voynich hums an affirmation. 'I still owe you though.'

Hare smiles and clutches the conker tight. 'You do. I won't forget. But try not to get eaten again, yeah?'

Voynich finds himself smiling too as he nods. 'Do my best. Be safe, Hare.'

They laugh and crouch to ruffle Pod, then watch as man and pig turn to trail around the pond and off through the grass, keeping to the shade of the trees.

Pod glances up at Voynich. He looks down at her and shrugs, so she trots onwards with her tail flicking happily.

2023 POETRY COMPETITION

Poetry Competition Judge's Report
Kirsten Norrie

It's always a great honour to be asked to judge a poetry prize, though prizes are necessarily strange and sometimes brutal situations. My truest instinct is that the notion of prize-giving attenuates a culture to what is excellent and permissible in the world of the written word. From Greek rhetorics to the Welsh Eisteddfod, poetry awards are an acknowledgement of skill, form and conviction and yet many of the submissions I received—and there were nine-hundred-and-thirty-seven, all of which I read with attention—were written from the heart. This heartedness which has chosen poetry as its locus, its place, is indicative of the era we are in. Lockdown poems of loneliness featured in the submissions list, as did desperate accounts of death: deaths of fathers, of foxes, of children, of the old, the sick and the lonely. It is a strange era to judge a prize in, when so many of the poems were judges themselves: of circumstance, of emotional neglect, of anti-governmental feeling, of tragedy and sorrow. These heartfelt markings of place and time were, and are, true markers of actual and poetic place, of real circumstance, which made the inability to longlist many of them deeply troubling to me. For those who aren't aware of the inner workings of a prize adjudication—and this will vary from prize to prize —many disqualifying elements manifest by dint of numbers and themes.

The downside to anonymous judging is that a poet can submit many entries and if their voice or style is not immediately recognisable, then several poems can be longlisted which have been mulled over and realigned in the mind of the judge many times. Longlists and shortlists serve to narrow, but these narrowings consist of choices: between form and feeling, for example. Many poems were very nearly longlisted and shortlisted. Poems recur in the mind and are reinstated, minutiae decide on whether one poem stays or goes and, the most peculiar of situations

—where a collective voice manifests, poems that are too similar in theme, suffer. My challenge was what to do when so many of those poems told of personal loss in the dark times we have just been through? If a great many poets are responding in this way, should a competitive element debar this collective voicing of grief? My other challenge was in selecting poems which represented a wide range of cultural voices: not the usual trope of diversity per se, but a tonal range that was complex in its making: a poetic culture of voicings. Whether these things can be separated is unlikely, and I don't have the room to expand on this here, but I was determined to locate a culture of poetics within the scope and range of my selection: poems that vivified form, that worked in counterpoint to one another. Poems which were aligned to enactments of place, that conjured and ventriloquised a spirited artistry; poems that did not necessarily concur to traditional form, that perhaps were instinctively aligned more to Olson than Paterson. And yet, craft remained crucial to the selection: who had housed the work in an excellence of prosody, a language beaten through its own devices. I'm not in full agreement with the glib actuations of 'passion' and 'story' that seem to trail so much of contemporary discourse around making— and I use making in its Scottish sense, in relation to the 'makar' the maker of poetry.

The performative ability of sonics and prosody to facilitate a live-wire within poetics, beyond narrative, beyond story, is a vital clue to poetry's own survival, I suspect. I also feel dispassionate about the intensive cultural rhetoric of 'loving' or being 'passionate' about the work, because—as a working poet, I know a considerable amount of poetry is graft and tensile; you grapple with the material and a versatile range of catalysts and inspirations force or guide or break your hand. I also feel Hemingway, as a big game hunter, necessarily killed his darlings—that was how he was wired up, and that sometimes the darling is the locus, the quiet, blue flame of a poem—the activation point to be worked and worried into existence: worried as in to quibble with fire, to get some friction going for ignition. These are gnostic touch points. Some poems carried a seed of their own irony, but this didn't over-ride a latent earnestness of condition or thought and perhaps set up a good sense of torsion between the two. Other poems chose to reference, rather coolly and possibly safely, the art historical. But there was an art to this also, a poised inflammation and a rhetoric of elegance. Some still could be polished into final position but carried a legacy of 'isness' they still kept a raw crudeness in the arc of their intent. A reduction to three is practically impossible: much swithering and redressing occurred. But, the three stand: they are complete and cast their own complicated shadows.

POETRY FIRST PRIZE

PANTOUM (after Béla Tarr)
Ben Howard

'It was as if the real threat came from elsewhere, from somewhere beneath their feet, though its source was bound to be uncertain: a man will suddenly find silence frightening, he fears to move.'
(LÁSZLÓ KRASZNAHORKAI, *Satantango*)

'To beguile the time, look like the time.'
(*Macbeth*)

Slush throbs on mildewed-soaked windowsills.

The cobwebs are arranged. These aeolians strung up
In a knotted stasis in crack and crevice.
Yet by whom. Never mind. Enter: their brother's distant keeper—Two scintillating
slits, a cold film of cobalt,

Whirling in a knotted stasis in crack and crevice,
Poised watchman, between walls that weep green of cabbage and communal slag.
Enter: another two smouldering slits, to watch over the grimed whirlwind
Of weathervane and choking isle. His webbed skull—

As it takes in the panorama between walls that weep of cabbage and shared slag,
—Is like a snowflake noting the slow patience of diplomacy,
Alighting whitely on weathervane and isle. The caretaker's slithering skull
Drips, softly, with creation, rising like damp, whilst

A suffocated snowflake notes the mounting insistence of diplomacy.
Her wind-struck wound a phosphorescence from the west sun.
His pulse drips, softly, rising like damp.
Tundra's gift. Thank you. The silencing leopard smothers

Her wind-struck wound, huffing and puffing from the west sun.
In the stewing November mire, a burin of clawed images are chiselled.
Tundra's alms. Bless you. The fugitive leopard dissolves
With the rain, pacing up and down, swigging pálinka outside their frontier.

In the cracked November mirror, an eyelid falls gently like a beaten wing
As the wooden bureaucrat clocks: *tick-tock, knock-knock, tick-tock, knock-knock.*
The rain paces up and down, downing pálinka just outside their arbour.
An imperial talon etches out our nailed-on hands, whilst

The cuckoo yacks: *tock-tick, knock-knock, tock-tick, knock-knock,*
Mumbling, soon enough, (lest fate evade it), the stink shall surely hit the fan,
Like an imperial talon stretching out nailed-on hands.
We ooze please from tipped hats. The rain broods, sparking up, outside our gate

Whilst the winking cock spoils the next act (the brown re-hitting the fan.)
So the prayers fester like lichen suckling the candle-dark altar,
As the rain shimmers outside and a choir of voices is bought to a steady simmer:
Inhuman Leviathan! You raise us, whilst you sink us; you move us, whilst we are muted

POETRY SECOND PRIZE

Counter Meals
Stephanie Powell

Down the local how beautiful the fellas are on Friday night
all machismo & handsome-haired
with beery smiles, cue tips slicing knuckle-melon, moving at the leisure
of a long unsuccessful game. More bankrupt, each pint-fattened hour
sways like new shoots in soft soil.

By savage junction footy boys slapping backsides, wrapping arms over necks
(St.) Peter—
sainted patron, local of locals, flapping jaw, body tented over the bar.

He'd had a mother to cook for him and was a choirboy
singing the lord's greatest hits –
    nearer my god to thee
etc. in high-voiced pureness, loving all the mezzo soprano angels
he was paid for weddings and funerals to sing sing as virgin
as cloudless winter.

Red wine birthmarks this front bar sideshow   declining in consciousness
sway like bullrushes, sways and melts like ice on a glass, like ghosts in rooms
like unfolding tendons.

The forking road, a bus wobbling down a prong. An earth digger
bathing in moonlight. Cordoned, cut dirt shines. Where is the driver?
Sunk into a cool frothy, a sea over the rock of back molars.

The meat lives in the freezer beside the chips and seafood special
a frozen farm with no cockerel, the residue of bitterest almond
mating foraged earth on the rim of the plate—
                              food not eaten with your hands.

This meal is progress acid in the nose dropped chips on the floor and
builders' hands that smell of deep, deep somewhere
south of midnight
north of no centre at all.

POETRY THIRD PRIZE

Ode to a Chimú Pot
Mark Fiddes

The exhibits are muttering in clay from the time rivers ran red
with Chimú blood and Cardinals.
One pot handle is a jaguar speaking through sharp incisors.
Ask what she has left
to guard after so many centuries of drought.
My thirst, she says.
It is best to thirst with all your heart so mountains melt for you.
Spill, she says.
Spill from your brim, down your slick terracotta skin
to tap roots at the Earth's core where each one of us is a seed
planted with love by an ancestor
because they too have a right to breathe.
Fill up with decades, she says.
Leave no room for ashes and don't scrape off the skim.
Spill, she says.
Spill from your brim, not still as a marble bride
but ravished and wet-tongued.
Make every day a sacrifice to the beast who devours the sun.
My truth is beauty only because you will always die for more.

Ars Poetica: 6pm
Louise Walker

After he dies suddenly at 24,
I fear that hour in winter
when streetlights provide
their harshest illumination, that hour
when people come home, begin
to think of supper, maybe pour a drink.

Each day I go to school, stand in front
of the class and write important words
like *assonance* and *alliteration* on the board,
then today's task: *How does the poet
explore the process of grief in this poem?*

Diligently the students choose quotations:
A hand that can be clasp'd no more—
and *on the bald street breaks the blank day.*

We squeeze the last tear from every word
and metaphor, until I come to a sudden
stop at the bleak monosyllables:
He is not here.

The class is silent, remembering
why I was away some weeks before—
and then we realise the task is done.

Back home, I plan the next day's lesson;
the distant roar of traffic summons

a familiar, indeterminate dread, until
at 6pm, a mother starts to call her son
in from the playground, drawing out
the vowels of his name like a lament,
as mothers call every night at 6pm,
that hour when boys come home for tea.

Autumn Wind
Jeanette Burney

always when the leaves turn spirals down from tree to ground and
the rough wind stirs the papers down from desk to floor the quiet
comes—

      suddenly the butcher lays the knife upon the bench
      and the aging woman ties her hair into a knot:
      they walk into the lifting night
      they turn toward the straining street
      but the grasses rise to meet them
      and the moon looks over the tenement roof
      and the soft noise of garbage under their feet
      becomes the leaves that follow the peddler's call
      in the ears of boys who shine men's shoes
      in the ears of women washing high above the street
      in the ears of those who slump and pick their teeth
      and lie in wait for the easy neon light
      of a city where trees are few and dying
      and the grass has forgotten the roaring field
      but here is the moon, that doesn't forget
      the two who witness changes in the broken glass—
      the eyes that see a thousand little stars along the curb
      the eyes that see a piecemeal cosmos in reflected light

always when the wind undoes the sound from where it came,
it speaks to those who wonder why they pause—
the man and woman turning circles in the street,
the writer bending over papers on the floor,
all hesitate to ask the question slipping out the door—
what quiet comes?

COLOR BLIND
Gina Shaffer

Y donde esta tu abuelita?
Where is your grandmother hiding?
Cinnamon skin beneath silky clothes,
She sits in stoic enchantment
Fanning herself in the summer breeze.

The question hangs unanswered
Smothered by shame and embarrassed shrugs
Silent traces of blood legacies left behind
A veil of island reveries seeing no distinctions.

Y donde esta tu abuelita?
Where is your grandmother hiding?
She kneels beneath an altar of indifference
Her voice muffled by fate and winds
If you listen closely, you might hear her tears.

End of an Afternoon
Donald Wildman

The waves rolling over in the
day's late sunlight are like
hills of evening spreading over the shore.

Briefly the light lies on the water.
The deep cold pulls at our feet, like a
net adrift in the day, its shadow glinting with fish.

All that's left is this gull-picked hour on the edge
of stillness, the low sun pouring through the dunes,
lighting the sea oats, warming our shoulders.

We are impelled, cement and all, toward the old water.
The earth rolls in the void, and the day is gone
like a meteor and its thread, like a father from his chair.

Night is coming over the ocean, its gray ships
silent on the horizon, its plumes of oblivion
all arrayed, its planet gleaming like a bell.

Homecoming
Amy Levitin Graver

I wrote a love poem for my first husband, Tyler, to read at his memorial service. There was much pain and too few answers surrounding his death. My heart has yet to heal. I am still trying to understand the choices he made that led him to be alone when he died. I sit listening to the minister as my mind begins to drift. We are back hiking in the Maine woods where he grew up. We would often sit together talking by the stream. He was so happy here. He is asking me if he can come home now. I try to make the running water flow backwards, but I cannot. I am startled at ceremony's end by the loud pealing of the bells. Tyler's two young nephews are pulling hard on the old ropes making them call out: Ka-klang, ka-klang, ka-klang. *Tyler is home. Tyler is home. Tyler is home.*

>autumn leaves falling
>letting go of the branches
>that held them so close

Otsuchi
Ben Verinder

Inagawa Sumiko picks up the disconnected phone and carefully dials his dead wife Mikayo. She takes a while to answer. 'How are you?' he asks. 'And what have you been doing with your days?' The wind lifts a wave of blossom from the cherry tree,
breaks it over the white booth, lilies, euphorbia. 'I sent a message but there was no answer,' he says, again. 'I listened to the radio and knew then how many of you had been swept away.' Along the path, past the wooden sign and through the turquoise arch, comes the orphan Toichiro Ishikawa. 'I'll take care of myself,' promises Sumiko. 'Just like I have since High School. I have to go. Goodbye.' A red lorry passes along the Sankiru Expressway at the end of the lane.

Life in a Hammershøi Painting: A study of parts
Lois P Jones

When we find figures in Hammershøi's interiors, they are like Hopper's figures, totally silent and static, entirely submissive to these immaculate rectilinear spaces. Poul Vad

1. *Hammershøi's Young Girl Sewing, 1887*
    I wonder how many ghosts can fit inside her. She needs no parchment
to map her design. If she laces anything out of loneliness it is a curtain revealing her lover's face
    in the crowd. So why should the modern world want to silence her hands? Women
    already catching their ankles in the rain, their shoulders bare at the window where their necks
    burn with erasure.
Women of mason jars rancid with fruit who have sewn too many fields.
    Women drunk from all-night parties and the memory of a man's
scent on their satin gowns. But who praises this figure bent over the needle and brushed
    into grainy silence? Whose arm embraces the waist below the dark brown bodice,
the skirt half shadowed in afternoon light? Art reorders the world, look at the way
    her brow determines the shape of it, the eyes holding the loose filament of cloth, still
translucent in her hands.

2. *Interior, Sunlight on the Floor, 1906*
Here is a poem like this Hammershøi painting. I read it again and hold its slender weight in my palm. The spare text: *exhumed* on a single line. I can set it next to the sliver of slate *taken* near Rilke's headstone. See how its light breathes down the nape of the neck. To write with such stasis requires a mind of the grave. How a body turns *away* toward the door, a woman's black dress unlatching its darkness.

3. *Rilke visits Hammershøi in Copenhagen*

"These women can only turn their backs on him—and yet he holds their sadness, speaking it with his blacks and greys and blues…—he gives himself to their silence. He is these women, whose breathing and whose meditation makes the room burn."

~*Nichola Deane's Imaginary Journal*

4. *Interior, 1899*

Sometimes a woman lands inside a scene and she can only turn her back on it. Faceless, she can be anyone—the wife whose mother grew mad as an abandoned garden. Only the erotic porcelain of her neck, the way light is born of its phosphine. You know it is her not because of the body, but the way spirit tilts the head on its axis   something fills the space around the mind—an intangible winter and its thoughts that walk on stilts. What holds her frame and presses from behind, pushing the length of her into the next room. Sometimes the walls are chalk white and the skirts speak their griege and Dutch blues. You try your future on like a pair of black stockings. You try it on. You tear it off.

Mythology
Ben Verinder

In my favourite story of a river
a man fishes a deep cold pool beside a bank
so steep a ladder rises from the surface
to the clover fields which late dusk
now obliviates, the evening quiet
as an empty hall, just the sound
of blackwater running and slow switch
of line in the dark, so dark it tastes
metallic, like a coin, the pool,
no matter what its name, nameless now,
then the sudden shock of splash,
a cry like a distant horn.

The man understands a calf
has fallen from the bank.
He rests his rod on the branch
of a willow, gently as one might hang
a lyre, his waistcoat like a fleece,
wades towards the gurgling, as if the beast
must disappear for him to grasp it,
lifts it onto his shoulders like a sack of grain,
stumbles towards the memory
of the ladder, bunches the hooves
in one hand as if swearing an oath,
and climbs, his strength ebbing
as a swimmer's but enough
to reach the highest rung, cross the pasture
and lay the calf before the bellows

of its mother, turn back to the river,
eyes adjusted. The man, who is my father,
descends and crosses over.

A RIVER RUNNING SHALLOW
After Mark Tredinnick
for Ellie
Kevin Smith

At the rear of the library, a bay window looks over
a river running shallow into a dry autumn. The water's

clear enough to find rocks lying in the river's bed, quilted
with brown slime and shadowed by a canopy of crow's ash

and rose gum. Whispered voices weave their way through
shelves of books—the way the water wends its way

among the rocks—as if searching for knowledge, for wisdom
embodied. The river is silent. A woman sits opposite me;

she's young enough to be my daughter. A year ago,
she asked if she could sit with me at a table outside a café.

It's how we met. I expected not to see her again. But here
she is, working hard the semester's last assignment.

She rises and goes to the window; she looks out, sees nothing
—her mind fraught. She tells me she had to take her son

to hospital last night, that his fever kept them there till four
in the morning. We watch through plated glass the river

tell the only truth it knows. A breeze drags branches of leaves
noiselessly across the water's surface. And a heron steps

with caution the current downstream. I catch the girl's
reflection in the glass. 'I want to see the end of this,'

she says. I picture the river dropping off the escarpment
and finding its way to the sea. Sure enough, it'll come back

to us as rain. Her eyes tell a tiredness only young mothers
know, a tiredness only weeks of uninterrupted sleep

could resolve. She returns to the table and resumes her work.
A quietness has settled in the library's aisles. And I, alone

again. And she, among her books, alone too. Along the river,
the heron steps through shadows that turn like pages.

2023 CYGNATURE POETRY PRIZE WINNER

Cygnature Poetry Prize Judge's Report
Sarah Davies

So, how to go about judging poetry? It's like deciding on the best cloud, or shade of blue, or my favorite note in music—yet it has to be done, at least when you're judging a competition. It's a difficult task, but it was a privilege. After some winnowing, I was left with a lot of good, serious poems that young people had obviously put a lot of thought into writing. So, how did I make my decision?

First of all, to find some common ground in the entries. Human experience is distinct, yet somehow fundamentally the same. There were a number of recurring themes and poems which bore a familial resemblance to each other, filtered through different sensibilities and lenses.

One theme I picked out, and which constituted a sizable proportion of entries, were poems of loss and of the search for identity. These were poems that examined trauma, but also moved the reader forwards. The anonymity of the authors was a great help here, and had me wondering— who had written which poem, whose experience was I reading about? There was a great deal of poetry as therapeutic model, and those that I found most successful were those that did not lose sight of the personal element but still made it 'Art', made it *poetry* rather than just confession. These moved from the specific to the universal and were poems which used the techniques of poetic skill to express and examine emotion.

Another theme of the submitted poems was the examination of difference—whether in culture, race, gender… Again, a constant subject was writers finding their place, their struggles doing so, and for some, a celebration of their achievement. There were also what some people might consider more 'typical' poetry themes represented—nature, landscape, etc. A lot of these I enjoyed, especially in their use of description and evocation.

I was surprised by the amount of formal poetry, of the use of form and metre, and especially by the use of rhyme. This was interesting, because I wasn't sure before starting to read the entries, if this demographic would use rhyme as a poetic device. However, I realised that, perhaps due to influence of spoken word etc. (where use of rhyme and metre can be a really effective tool) that this was a popular choice. Of course, rhyming can be two-edged sword, as can metre. Poets run the risk of being constrained by their own choices. However, there were many that used these effectively as strategies and were the better for it.

What are common mistakes that can spoil a poem? Well, for me as a poet, the common mistakes I, and others, make are many. One is being too attached to what the poem starts out as, and not seeing it through to where it's going. There are poems that start strong and peter out. There are poems that, (while I don't always mind telling as well as showing), start to become one–note. There are poems that confuse complex language with sophistication, when simplicity may be more effective and affecting. The poem doesn't always need to have a signposted and bravura ending, but it must have an end. The reader must be given space in the poem, and the poem must have its own inner logic and clarity.

So, what makes a prize-winning poem? looked at entries in terms of subject matter, individuality, technical issues and the inevitable, ineffable' je ne sais quoi'. Once the winnowing down was done, I had my different piles, which I crosschecked and re-read, noting down such things as the overall structure of the poem, use of language, meaning, consistency, shape, the poem as a whole *thing*.

The poems in my last ten were all good and I liked all of them for different reasons. Indeed, comparison was difficult. But what choosing the final few came down to was the gut feeling I had while reading them, the fact that I remembered them after I'd read them.

So why this poem? I liked its tone, its diction and theme. It stood out in many ways from other entries and had its own distinct voice. I had read a lot of first-person poems, and this was different. I hadn't read any other work with similar subject matter, which made it memorable and had me returning to it. I was intrigued by it and its story and what it was saying. I liked that it told a story and led us through this, leaving us to draw our own meanings and parallels, reminding me of how we read myths and how myths make us. It even begins like a story:

> *'There was a king once, and*
> > *He was*
> *So scared that breathing,'*

There are echoes of lessons repeated and unlearned from history:

> > *'What is our history*
> *But millennia stretched to dry across the axiom*
> > *You can't control everything,*
> > *Piled year, after*
> > *Year, after year.'*

After much deliberation, I was proud to award first prize to the poem, *Ashur Acha Iddina.*

Ashur Acha Iddina
Adam Ali-Hassan

There was a king once, and
> He was
So scared, that breathing

Through his teeth
He killed
The men in the throne room
> And in the passageway, and then
The men who were standing in
The temple, fingertips to their god.

The one who has all the power
> Has nothing to fear,
So he clearly didn't have all the power.
Indeed, sources tell us

> The poor bastard could feel gentle
Thunder scattering
The anxious little bones
In his feet for lots,
As foundation stones he'd watched wedding mortar
> Solved and dissolved down
Away in the darkness. Then, then now, again he'd loathe

> *Ashur Acha Iddina would loathe*
> His skin of sweat even after he'd set
> Block of limestone
Between himself and the world

After block after block. And no
Matter how
      Tightly he twisted
His fingers, bleeding swollen into
Bloodshed, he would hold onto his sceptre and feel
      Its shattering written on his
Viscera, there. For
                What is our history
But millennia stretched to dry across the axiom
      You can't control everything,
      Piled year, after
      Year, after year.

2023 BEDFORD POETRY PRIZE WINNER

Bedford Poetry Prize Judge's Report
Liam Coles

The crop of poems I was asked to judge for this competition was an excellent harvest. We had several poems inspired by local places in the Bedford area, which was pleasing to see as a Bedfordian. I gravitated towards poems with some form, that were not just unrefined outpourings of feelings. Though of course, high feelings are a key source of poetry, too, and it was a privilege to read of the passions that stir local poets. But, as Larkin said of Hardy's poetry, poems need a 'spine'—a conceit that makes them into a formed aesthetic object. This is not to say that traditional poetic forms must be used, although I read two excellent villanelles, but that the form of the poem should interact with, comment on, or enhance its themes and contents somehow. The poem I have chosen as winner is: *Mothering Sunday: At the "Garden of Rest"*.

This elegiac sonnet recounts a trip to a graveyard to visit the poet's mother's grave. The images of burgeoning life at the outset are juxtaposed with the sombre setting: the darting squirrel; the tree shaking gold from its hair; the caressing mist (affording the mist an active, loving role), and even the cold which is dewy dappled, glinting with life and hope. We are reminded that this is a 'garden' of rest—amongst death is the possibility of new beginnings, of another spring. Even the bench is 'fresh' deserted: and this move into remembering her mother's perspective is well-handled: her kind imagined attitude to the person who has slept on the bench (perhaps a rough sleeper) tells us something about her character. In fact, this kindness illuminates the poem like spring sunshine.

Grief responses are deftly sketched—the widower scared his wife is cold is a particularly moving memory. And the poem ends on a jarring note. The daughter forgets: does she forget where the plot is? Or does she forget to lay flowers one year? It's a disquieting *volta*, whose sadness is offset by the tracing of the garden at the start of the poem.

I was impressed to read so formally realised a poem. It's an English or Shakespearean sonnet, marked out by its rhyme scheme, its three quatrains, and that concluding couplet. Sonnets were called by Dante Rossetti a 'moment's monument' and the moment this sonnet memorialises is both lonely and full of life, grief-stricken and contemplative, sad but also tender.

Mothering Sunday: At the "Garden of Rest"
Anne Atkins

The day is aching here with loneliness.
A squirrel darts and stops; the tree shakes gold
Out of its hair; the morning mists caress
The stones, the yew, the dewy dappled cold.
That bench looks fresh deserted: someone slept
Here, while the distant traffic snored awake.
You would have given him that kindness kept
Within your smile for all; so for your sake
I'm glad he found rest here. And what of you?
My father cried out in his dreams, with fear
That you were cold; the bitter rains soaked through
That cruel winter that we left you here.
      I memorised each blade to mark the plot
      To lay my flowers for you. And then forgot.

Biographies

Adam Ali-Hassan lives in London but is currently studying Ancient Near Eastern at Oxford, and he is in his final year of undergraduate study. Although he has been living in the UK for many years now, he is half Belgian and half Bruneian by birth, and he spent his childhood in Singapore. He has been writing poetry, mostly as a private hobby, for quite a while now, but his work has evolved as he has gotten more and more practise. Poetry is not an isolated aspect of what he does but one closely tied to his everyday life and to his love of languages, cultures, and philosophy.

Other than writing, he enjoys spending time listening to music. When he leaves the academic world, he may go into journalism, but currently busy he is preparing for finals.

Anne Atkins is primarily a novelist, also award-winning journalist, columnist, playwright, lyricist and broadcaster as well as poet. Her novels include, *An Elegant Solution,* set in Cambridge, *The Lost Child, On Our Own* and *A Fine and Private Place.* The next in the current trilogy, *Never Too Late,* is in progress.

She has written for all major national British newspapers including weekly columns in *The Telegraph* and *Daily Express* as well as household-name magazines; presented for Channel 5, ITV and BBC and is perhaps best known for her *Thoughts for the Day* on Radio 4's flagship *Today* programme.

Her play, *Lady K,* was scheduled to run at the Theatre Royal, Windsor in 2020, but was cancelled due to lockdown. She worked as an actor (most recently at the National Theatre and founded the *Shakespeare Players)* before writing full-time.

In 2020 her *Anthem for Mary and David,* set to music by her son, Ben Atkins, was featured in tv and radio programmes and published by Encore Publications. It can be found on YouTube, as can her song, *Can the Sky Forget Rain,* with composer Caroline Leighton.

Mothering Sunday: at the "Garden of Rest" was written for her mother, Mary, for whom no words can ever be enough.

Chris Belson is a writer of short fiction, poetry and song, living in Bedford. He has a Masters in Creative Writing from The Open University, his work has been published in *Popshot* magazine, and his music has been played on national BBC radio.

His work often explores the blurry, dream-like borders between psychological and physical space, and the particular, flawed lenses through which we each see the world around us. He is currently working on further short stories and developing his first novel.

Jeanette Burney is a poet, teacher and lawyer from San Antonio, Texas. Previously, she lived in Austin, Houston, Munich and San Francisco. A longtime vegetarian and singer of sacred music, she collects stray dogs and cats. Previously, her poetry has appeared in more than a dozen literary magazines including *Shenandoah*, *The Minnesota Review*, *Acumen* and *Poetry Australia*. In 2023, her poem, *Introduction to the Kitchen*, won the Hastings Poetry Festival Prize.

Joy Clews lives in a small village in Lincolnshire. Many of her writing ideas develop as she walks and cycles the county's countryside and coast.

Although her academic studies and early career focussed on mathematics, Joy has always been passionate about literature and the potential of stories to change lives. A decision to make the transition from full-time work as a senior manager in the university sector to more flexible educational consultancy work gave her the opportunity to write fiction. Her writing portfolio now includes short stories, flash fiction, a novel and a ghost-written memoir.

Joy was awarded first place in the Flash 500 short story competition and second place in the Frome Festival competition. She was shortlisted for the Bridport Short Story Prize, the Bridport Flash Fiction Prize and the Writing Magazine and Henshaw Press short story competitions. Her writing has been highly commended and longlisted in seven other competitions.

Joy is currently editing her second novel.

Tony Durrant, on leaving university, trained as a print journalist, working as a news reporter across the North of England. While on the Daily Mirror, in London, he escaped to the wild places when he could, qualifying as a mountain leader, hiking and climbing throughout the UK and the Alps.

As a freelance journalist he covered the rise of adventure sports, contributing to outdoor lifestyle magazines, but mostly the Daily Telegraph for which he also wrote a health and fitness column. He taught yoga on the side, encouraged by the surgeon who sorted out his spine (a parachuting legacy).

Work took him to many places, including Afghanistan in 2012 and 2014, where he had the idea for *A Dying Breed*. He studied for an MA in Creative Writing with the Open University and has had work shortlisted in the Wilbur Smith Adventure Writing Award 2020 and the Page Turner Awards, 2023. Tony lives in the Pennine Hills of Cumbria with Sally and their Labradors, Harper and Fizz.

Mark Fiddes lives and works in the Middle East. His latest collection of award-winning poems, *Other Saints Are Available,* (Live Canon) follows *The Rainbow Factory* and *The Chelsea Flower Show Massacre,* (both Templar). Over the past year, work has appeared in Shearsman Magazine, Stand, The North, Oxford Poetry, The Moth, Oxford Poetry, The Irish Times and has been anthologized in the Forward Book of Poetry and 'Masculinity' (Broken Sleep). He's a winner of the Oxford Brookes University International Prize, the Ruskin Prize, the Westival Prize and a runner up in the Bridport Prize and National Poetry Competition among many others. He has recently appeared at the Versopolis Poetry Expo '24 in Ljubljana and the Emirates Literary Festival in Dubai.

Isaac Hogarth is 22 years old, and lives in Sydney, Australia. He developed a voracious appetite for reading as a child, though lost this somewhat over the years; during the dark days of COVID, however, Isaac rediscovered his love for literature and has been writing diligently ever since. The Bedford Competition is the first literary prize he has won (but hopefully not the last!). Isaac is fascinated with transience and meeting points; the spaces where light intersects with dark, laughter with crying, and misery with joy. He is currently finishing his undergraduate studies at University of Sydney, majoring in Literature and Studies in Religion. In future, Isaac hopes to write for a living in some capacity; any capacity, really.

Ben Howard is a poet who grew up in Leeds but has been living in China as an English teacher with his beautiful supporting wife for the past 8 years. He has been working on his first poetry collection for around 6 years, which aims to blend the historical with the personal, the spaces where the towers of the city crumble into us.

Lois P Jones won the 2023 Alpine Fellowship which took place in Fjällnäs, Sweden. Other awards include the Bristol Poetry Prize, the Lascaux Poetry Prize and the Tiferet Poetry Prize. She was a winning finalist for the Terrain Poetry contest, a finalist in 2023 for the annual Mslexia Poetry Competition, and in 2022 for the Best Spiritual Literature Award in Poetry from Orison Books. Other honors include a Highly Commended and publication in the 2021 Bridport Poetry Prize Anthology. Jones' work appears or is forthcoming in the *Academy of American Poets – Poem A Day, Poetry Wales, Mslexia, Plume, Agenda, Guernica Editions, Vallentine Mitchell of London; Image, Verse Daily*, and others. Her first collection, *Night Ladder,* (Glass Lyre Press) was a finalist for the Julie Suk Award. In collaboration with filmmaker Jutta Pryor and sound designer Peter Verwimp, Lois' poem *La Scapigliata* won the 2022 Lyra Bristol Poetry Film Competition. She was a screening judge for Claremont University's Kingsley-Tufts Awards from 2018-2022. Since 2007 Jones has hosted KPFK's Poets Café, and acts as poetry editor for the Pushcart prize-winning Kyoto Journal.

David Joseph is a recipient of The Paul Cave Prize for Literature, Independent Press Award, and the Next Generation Indie Book Award. His writing has been published in The Wall Street Journal, LA Times, London Magazine, The Smart Set, Litro, and Rattle. He is the author of three collections of short fiction—*The Old Men Who Row Boats and Other Stories, I Didn't Know What To Say So I Just Said Thanks* and *I*

Never Knew How Old I Was. graduate of Hobart College and the University of Southern California's Graduate Writing Program, he was a recipient of the Kerr Fellowship and served as editor for the Southern California Anthology. In 2002 he cofounded the non-profit organization America SCORES LA, and in 2007 he received The John Henry Hobart Fellowship for Ethics and Social Justice. He has taught at Pepperdine University and Harvard University. In 2019, he was awarded a position on the Fulbright Specialist Roster. He lives in Andalucía, Spain with his wife Karen.

Dell Kaniper has a Master's in Creative Writing from the New School and a Bachelor's in Theatrical Literature from Ithaca College. Her fiction has appeared in print and online in Narrative Magazine, Vine Leaves Press. She is a recipient of a grant from the Artist Trust (2021) and has had short fiction named a semi-finalist in American Fiction's Halifax Ranch Fiction Prize.

She currently works as a copywriter and splits her time between Seattle, Washington, and Oaxaca de Juarez, Oaxaca, Mexico.

Daniel Key is from London, England. He has a MA in Creative Writing from Birkbeck, University of London. He writes a poem every day, even if it's a bad one, but he most enjoys writing short stories. His work has appeared in the Meniscus Literary Journal, Quibble Lit and is forthcoming in Mojo magazine. Find him on Twitter @danielkey0.

Sheila Killian is an award-winning author who lives in Limerick on the west coast of Ireland with her family. She has published poetry and short fiction *in Smokelong Quarterly, Brevity, The Ogham Stone, The Shop, Electric Acorn, Aerial* and, *Revival.* Her first novel, *Something Bigger,* was published in 2001. She has won awards for short fiction, poetry, and travel writing, and has also published a wide range of non-fiction academic work, including two books. She has taught creative writing as part of the UL Creative Writing Winter School programmes, and acted as a writing mentor with Walls of Limerick, an initiative to support writers from less-represented communities.

Sheila has also published a wide range of academic work including peer-reviewed papers, some in translation, and two published books. Her creative non-fiction has been broadcast on Ireland's national radio station, RTE Radio One and her poetry has been anthologised by The Liffey Press in Ireland and Aerial in South Africa. She is a professional member of the Irish Writers Centre and the Irish Writers Union.

She is currently working on a second novel and a first collection of short stories, and she spends as much time as she can by the sea.

Amy Levitin Graver is working on completing her debut poetry collection for publication. Her award-winning poetry is featured in Central Avenue's anthology collection released in April 2024. Amy has also served as a judge for several prestigious poetry contests, including NFSPS and the Pennsylvania Poetry Society. Currently, she holds the positions of Executive Secretary and Youth Chair at the Connecticut Poetry Society, channeling her passion for poetry into initiatives for local students. Notably, she created a program called "Art Fusion," which is an ekphrastic poetry project at the Educational Center for the Arts, a New Haven arts magnet school. Amy played a pivotal role in establishing the Poet Laureate position in her hometown of Branford, Connecticut. Additionally, she is creating Branford's first anthology and workshop project collaboratively with her town's counseling center, leveraging poetry to aid in trauma and PTSD recovery—a cause she is deeply committed to advocating.

Stephanie Powell is a poet based in Melbourne. Her latest collection is *Gentle Creatures* (Vagabond Press, 2023). Her poetry can be found in Rabbit, Cordite, Island Magazine, The Suburban Review, Victorian Writer, Mascara Literary Review (Resilience Anthology), Acumen, The Rialto, Ambit Magazine, Bad Lilies, The Moth and Poetry Wales. In September 2024 her new collection, Small Acts, will be published by Liquid Amber Press.

Felicity (Fil) Reid, who has Asperger's Syndrome, has been writing all her life. However, life got in the way in the shape of various jobs, her horses, and her family. She's run a riding school from her arable farm in Berkshire, farmed sheep in Pembrokeshire, run holiday cottages in

Brittany and lived in a canal boat. But now she's happier than ever in Cornwall, where her next books with Dragonblade, out from June 2024, and set in the Regency period, take place.

She won the Dragonblade Publishing Write Stuff Competition in 2021, with a three-book deal that's led to books four to six being published in her successful six book *Guinevere Series*. The *Guinevere* books were helped by King Arthur having been her lifelong Aspie obsession, alongside horses, so she already had all the research at the tips of her fingers.

Her short stories have been placed in the Creative Writing Ink Competition and the Canterbury SaveAsWriters Competition, and one of her children's books was third in the Wells Literary Festival Children's Book Competition.

When she's not writing she likes to sew for her grandchildren, read, and research all things historical.

Gina Shaffer, a Cuban American playwright and poet, has written several plays that have been staged throughout Southern California and off-Broadway. Inspired by her family history, *Under the Cuban Moon* was presented in a staged reading at Repertorio Español in New York City as a finalist in the MetLife Nuestras Voces National Playwriting Competition. *War Spelled Backwards*, a one-act play, was published in *The Literary Experience*, an anthology used in college classrooms. Other works include *Prufrock in the Park*, staged by Wayward Artists in Santa Ana, CA; *Dreaming of Barbie*, featured in the Last Frontier Theatre Conference in Alaska; and *If Memory Serves*, presented as part of a New Playwrights One-Act Festival at The Producers Theatre in New York. A graduate of UC Irvine, where she received a Ph.D. in English, Gina formerly was a faculty member at UCLA Writing Programs. In addition to teaching creative writing, literature, and composition as a professor of English at Saddleback College in Mission Viejo, CA, she serves as faculty advisor of WALL Literary Journal, an award-winning campus publication. Gina is a member of the Alliance of Los Angeles Playwrights and the Dramatists Guild.

Kevin Smith has worked as a teacher, writer, actor, and workshop facilitator in theatres, schools and universities. Two collections of his poetry have been published: *Awake to the Rest of My Days* (2021) was developed via a mentorship with Mark Tredinnick, administered by Australian Writers' Mentors. His second collection, *Another Day* was published in 2023 by Flying Islands Press.

In 2023 he won the $15,000 first prize in the prestigious Newcastle Poetry Prize, Australia, with his poem, *The Crossing*. In 2022, he placed 2nd in The Australian Catholic University Poetry Prize, and shortlisted in The Newcastle Poetry Prize, and The Bridport Prize.

His poems have featured in competitions abroad as well, including The Bridport Prize, The Fish Poetry Prize, The Robert Graves Poetry Prize, The Welsh International Poetry Prize, The Oxford Brookes International Poetry Prize, and The Bedford Competition.

Night Heron Under a Crescent Moon was shortlisted in the 2021 Fish Poetry Prize, County Cork, Ireland.

A third collection of poems—*She, The Boy Monk (The Cancer Poems)*—will be published by Birdfish Books in 2024.

Victoria Stewart was born in Crosby and lived in Sheffield, Leeds, Bristol and Leicester before moving back to Merseyside in 2021. Formerly a lecturer in English Literature, she now works as a researcher. Victoria has had work longlisted for the Lucy Cavendish Fiction Prize, the Bridport Novel Prize, and the Aurora Short Story Prize. Her flash fiction has been published online by Reflex and LISP, and in Ellipsis Zine and Restore to Factory Settings: Bath Flash Fiction Anthology 5.

Josie Turner lives in Kent and worked for the UK's National Health Service for over twenty years. Her prose and poetry have appeared in journals including The Four-Faced Liar, Brittle Star, The North, Gordon Square Review, Mslexia, Magma and Scoundrel Time. She has won the Brighton Prize for fiction and the Welsh Poetry Prize, and in 2024 her 100-word flash won the National Flash Fiction Day competition.

Ben Verinder lives in rural Hertfordshire. His debut pamphlet, *Botanicals*, was published by Frosted Fire in autumn 2021 and his second, *We Lost The Birds*, by Nine Pens in March 2023. His first collection, *How to save a river/father*, is a celebration of those who work to protect and restore rivers and was completed in late 2023. Ben is the biographer of the adventurer and writer Mary Burkett and a graduate of Newcastle University's Writing Poetry MA.

Louise Walker taught English for 35 years. Her poems have appeared in anthologies by the Sycamore Press and Emma Press, as well as journals such as South, Oxford Magazine, Acumen, and Prole. She was Highly Commended in the Frosted Fire Firsts Award in 2022; in 2023 she was long listed by The Alchemy Spoon Pamphlet Competition and won 3rd prize in the Ironbridge Poetry Competition. Commissions include Bampton Classical Opera and she collaborated with Gill Wing Jewellery on their showcase, *Poetry in Ocean'* Her new chapbook will be published by Dithering Chaps later in the year. Find her on Instagram @louise_walker_poetry

James Watson is a novelist and short story writer based in Dorset. Formerly an international lawyer, he was raised in the UK but has lived in Sub-Saharan Africa and Japan and has travelled extensively. His interest in different cultures informs his writing and his short stories seek to bring out the simple ironies of the human experience. He is currently working on a series of historical novels set in Egypt at the outbreak of the second world war; a cauldron of British martial might and burgeoning indigenous nationalism.

Lucia Wilde was born and educated in Bedford, finding a love of reading and then writing whilst in school. They also enjoyed involvement with theatre and music during this time before moving on to study English Literature and Drama at the University of Sussex. Although struggling with mental health during their degree, they graduated and spent some time trying to work out what on earth to actually *do*. Whilst the answers haven't been forthcoming, they have since returned to Bedford and now work as Deputy Manager of Oxfam Books & Music in Bedford. So, they're using that degree. Sometimes. They still read, and write, and attend the Read Poets society in the Eagle

Bookshop at the start of every month. Inspiration comes from anywhere and everywhere: the poems read at the society, work, conversations, other books, games of *Dungeons & Dragons* or creating stories with friends online. They have never written to be published before, aside from a short story that won an internal competition at university. Mostly, they just write for their own pleasure, and find it a joy if that writing reaches others. There may still be volumes of adolescent poetry locked away on various computers that will never see the light of day, but if there are we'll never know.

Donald Wildman grew up in Fairmont, West Virginia, along the banks of the Monongahela River in the western foothills of the Appalachian Mountains. He earned a B.A. in English and an M.A. in English from West Virginia University.

He is a retired English Instructor, having worked most of his career at Wake Technical Community College in Raleigh, North Carolina.

He was one of the founders, and the second president, of the North Carolina Community College Faculty Association, which lobbied the N.C. General Assembly for increased community college funding. He published point-of-view articles on faculty salaries in the Wilmington Star, the (Raleigh) News & Observer, the Durham Herald, the Charlotte Observer, and the Asheville Citizen-Times.

His poem, *Coming into Winter,* was a Finalist in the Atlanta Review International Poetry Contest and was published in their fall 2023 issue.

His poem, *End of an Afternoon,* was started many years ago on a beach in South Carolina and was recently revised.

Gwen Williams lives in Wales. She has been a social worker and a care home inspector for the Welsh Assembly. Her poetry has appeared in Poetry Wales, Spring Issue 59.3, 2024 and previously in The North and various anthologies. Currently she is writing a bilingual pamphlet of poetry about the Welsh settlers in Patagonia.

Her novel, *Somewhere to Go,* was long listed for the Bridport Prize in 2024—an extract was published in the Novel Anthology. She is aiming to complete the novel this year. She wrote a piece in Welsh for the book Merched Peryglus/Dangerous Women (pub.Honno, 2023)—a collection of the experiences of female activist members of Cymdeithas yr Iaith Gymraeg, one of the societies promoting the Welsh language.

Her late cousin who died during the pandemic, inspired the character of Lizzie in *Song from a Different Room*. From the age of four she spent forty-five years in an institution because she was undiagnosed as autistic and didn't speak. She was the most stoical person in any meeting and communicated non-verbally with power.

 **The Bedford Competition**

The Bedford Competition 2024

Share your words with us and the world

We invite you to submit stories up to 3000 words and poems up to 40 lines long

Prizes
1st £1500   2nd £300   3rd £200

Judges
Short Story— Liv Maidment
Poetry—Jessica Mookherjee
Cygnature Short Story Prize (17-25 yrs)—Stephen Bywater
Cygnature Poetry Prize (17-25 yrs)—Rishi Dastidar
Bedford Short Story Prize—Paul Barnes
Bedford Poetry Prize—Liam Coles

(Both Cygnature Prizes are sponsored by the University of Bedfordshire)

The Bedford Competition is a nonprofit group. All net proceeds this year will go to funding writing courses for local writers and helping literary-leaning charities.

Competition opens 1st May and closes 31st October 2024

To enter visit our website:
www.bedfordwritingcompetition.co.uk

Made in the USA
Columbia, SC
07 November 2024